CH00594634

THE SQUARE LEOPARD

THE
SQUARE
LEOPARD

Peter Miller

FREDERICK MULLER LIMITED
LONDON

First published in Great Britain 1980
by Frederick Muller Limited, London, NW2 6LE

Copyright © 1980 Peter Miller
Produced for television by HTV Ltd.

All rights reserved. No part of this publication may be
reproduced or transmitted in any form or by any means,
electronic or mechanical, including photocopying,
recording, or any information storage or retrieval system,
without prior permission in writing from the Publishers.

British Library Cataloguing in Publication Data

Miller, Peter
    The Square Leopard
    I. Title
    823'.9'1F   PR6063.I37/

    ISBN 0-584-31080-3

Typeset by Texet, Leighton Buzzard, Bedfordshire
Printed in Great Britain by The Anchor Press Ltd.,
Tiptree, Essex

Chapter One

The Family Upstairs

All along the pavement outside the Lampert family's house, people were twisting, turning and flattening themselves against garden walls. If you'd been there, you'd have done the same thing for nothing and nobody was safe when young Toby Lampert took to the pavement on his bike.

One by one, as they heard danger crank noisily past them, the pedestrians breathed out, opened their eyes and glared after the tousled seven-year-old pedalling furiously away from them. Suddenly, there was a screech of brakes, and they watched, horrified, as he skidded round the gate post in true dirt-track fashion, and collided with the man who was just entering the passage leading up to the house. He was a nervous, prim little man and was visibly shaking as he picked himself up and brushed the dirt from his well pressed trousers.

"I'm not allowed to ride on the road," Toby explained, as he clambered off his bike.

"You shouldn't be allowed to ride anywhere at that speed," the little man snorted.

Toby grinned sheepishly, turned away and trundled his bike up to the front door, leaving the angry little man to tut and fret his way behind.

The house, which was called The Laurels, was a semi-detached, three-storey building with a sedate Victorian look; and the street in which it stood formed one side of a sedate Victorian square, one of the quietest squares in the whole of Bristol. At least, that is how the residents of the square remembered it, before the tranquillity of the neighbourhood was shattered by the arrival of the

Lamperts in their midst.

The little man was peering at the large plaque on the front door of the house. It read:

GERALD PARISH

Solicitor

He jabbed the nameplate with his finger as he ranted on at Toby.

"Your father's a solicitor . . . but lets you terrorise the neighbourhood like that?"

Toby sniffed disdainfully.

"My father's dead." He nodded in the direction of the plaque. "He just rents the ground floor of our house." His tone made it clear that he didn't think much of Mr Gerald Parish, Solicitor, or of the fact that the Lampert family had to live above him.

He pushed the front door open, wheeled his bike inside and propped it against the wall just inside the door. The little man followed him into the hall and gazed, open-mouthed, as Toby began to negotiate the forest of greenery that adorned the stairs leading to the Lamperts' part of the house. There were plants on almost every step; plants dangling from the landing; plants trailing their abundant growth up and over and through the banisters. They were the pride and joy of Toby's eleven-year-old sister Joanna and they flourished under the green-fingered care she lavished on them, but they were a serious obstruction to anyone attempting to climb the stairs. The little man blinked in blank amazement as Toby disappeared among the foliage almost as though he were vanishing into the heart of an Amazonian jungle. He stood for a moment at the foot of the stairs, shaking his head slowly in disbelief, then turned and followed the directions of the notice in the hall to Gerald Parish's office at the end of the corridor, tapped on the door and entered.

"Good morning! My name's Fox!" he announced.

The thin, nervous-looking lady behind the desk, looked up from her knitting and waited for him to continue.

"I have an appointment to see Mr Parish!" he glanced anxiously at his watch. "I'm a few minutes early, actually."

Nesta Wright's lips cracked into a faint professional smile.

"Mr Parish has just popped out to do some shopping. He won't be long." She nodded her head grotesquely in the direction of a chair. "Would you care to take a seat . . . ?"

At that very moment, Gerald Parish was just returning from the shops with a large carrier bag full of groceries in his arms. Not having a free hand, he turned his back on the front door, pushed it open with his bottom and entered the house backwards. Unhappily, the door yielded a little too readily and he fell backwards, crashing with considerable force into Toby's bike, which was propped up against the wall behind the door. The mighty crash and the yell of terror which followed brought Nesta and Mr Fox rushing out into the hall. They stopped, aghast at what they saw.

Gerald was lying on his back, struggling to extricate his right leg from the tangled spokes of the wheel of the bike. Groceries were lying everywhere, with sugar from the burst packets spilling over the smoked salmon and gourmet foods so near to Gerald's heart.

His ever-faithful secretary and Mr Fox just stood and stared open-mouthed, and it was some moments before Nesta found her voice.

"Oh, Mr Parish! Have you had an accident?"

Gerald glared up at her and, if looks could have killed, she would surely have expired that very moment.

"No, Nesta! I'm practicing breaking my neck!" he snapped testily, as he finally yanked his leg free from the wheel and struggled to his feet. Breathing heavily, he turned round and surveyed the tangled wreckage behind him, and in a sudden frenzy launched a furious kick at the undamaged front wheel.

The shattering of the spokes brought an angry yell from the top of the stairs.

"You've bust my bike!"

Gerald groaned inwardly as he looked up and saw the tousled head of young Toby Lampert, bobbing in and out of the foliage as he picked his way among the plant pots, coming down the stairs. He was suddenly aware of the bewildered-looking stranger standing next to Miss Wright. She hastened to explain.

"Oh, this is Mr Fox, for his eleven o'clock appointment!"

"Oh, fine!" Gerald replied, forcing a smile to his ruffled features. "If you'd care to wait in my office, I won't keep you a moment."

As Nesta began to gather up the spilled groceries, he shepherded his perplexed client down the corridor towards his office. He was only just in time, for as he returned to the scene of the crime, he was at once set upon by the irate seven-year-old who had come down the stairs.

"You bust it!" he yelled. "You did it on purpose!"

"You left it there on purpose!" Gerald fumed back. "That's the third time I've nearly broken my neck on it this month!"

Toby wasn't in the least concerned about Gerald's neck. He could only think of his wrecked bike.

"Well, you're going to pay to get it mended!" he shouted.

"Oh, no!" Gerald laughed maliciously. "You're going to have to save up for that out of your pocket money. Perhaps that will teach you a lesson!"

Momentarily dejected, Toby turned and slowly began to ascend the stairs. After a couple of steps, his courage returned and he pushed his head through the foliage and shouted defiantly:

"I'm allowed to park my bike in the hall!"

"It doesn't say so in the lease your mother signed!" Gerald smirked.

"You tricked her into signing that!" Toby muttered.

Gerald didn't seem to hear him. He was on his home

4

ground now, and on legal matters was more than a match for a precocious seven-year-old.

"It specifically states . . ." he beamed with the superior air of the man who knows he's right, ". . . that the hallway must be left clear of all obstacles by both parties . . ." He broke off suddenly and frowned. "Tricked her? What do you mean, I tricked her?"

Toby glowered at him sullenly over the bannisters.

"All those wherefores and things. I couldn't understand it!"

"You couldn't understand it?" Gerald threw back his head and roared with laughter. "It wasn't designed to be in the same syllabus as Enid Blyton! I don't expect a seven-year-old boy to . . ." he suddenly broke off and his expression changed to one of anguish. He banged his head despairingly with his fist. "A seven-year-old! I'm standing here arguing with a rude, bad-tempered seven-year-old!"

Toby's head reappeared through the leaves.

"It's you that's always bad-tempered!"

"I have a right to be bad-tempered!" Gerald shouted up the stairs. "I have to suffer . . . day in and day out, I have to suffer five . . . repeat five maniac children who should all be locked up in some institution until they've learned to behave like human beings."

"You could always leave!" Toby suggested, innocently.

"And break my word?" He shook his head, smiling hypocritically up at the face in the foliage. "My lease has another five years to run and as a man of honour, I wouldn't dream of breaking my written word to your mother." He turned away, satisfied that he'd had the last word with this troublesome boy, when a voice shrieked out from the top of the stairs.

"The only reason you stay here is because you got it cheap!"

Gerald swung round sharply and glared up the stairs with a wild look in his eyes. He could cheerfully have murdered the boy, but Toby was no longer there, for having delivered his parting shot, he'd darted up the stairs to the safety of the family home.

With a great effort of will, Gerald pulled himself together and suppressed the desire to chase up the stairs and chastise his young tormentor . . . such behaviour would be quite unbecoming in a respectable professional man. He took in several deep breaths, straightened himself to his full height, and strutted down the corridor to attend to the client waiting in his office.

"Sorry to have kept you waiting, Mr Fox," he said, closing the door behind him. He crossed to his desk, sat down and carefully realigned the calendar, pen-tray and papers before clasping his hands together and beaming professionally over the desk at his client. "Now! What's the problem?"

Mr Fox fidgeted nervously on the edge of his chair.

"Well . . . it's probably going to sound rather silly really . . ."

Gerald waited for some moments for his client to continue, before suggesting:

"Is it something that's bothering you? . . . Worrying you?"

Mr Fox leaned forward earnestly and confided:

"It's driving me mad!"

"Well!" Gerald laughed. "There's nothing rather silly about that! Now what exactly is it, Mr Fox?"

Mr Fox paused momentarily, before replying in a half whisper.

"A cat!"

Gerald wondered if his ears were deceiving him.

"A cat?" he repeated.

Mr Fox drew his chair closer to the desk and began to talk excitedly.

"Don't know where it comes from but you see . . . my wife likes to sit out in the garden when it's warm and every time she does, this flaming great cat appears and jumps on her lap."

Gerald's concentration faltered momentarily as the faint but unmistakable sound of a pop record began to filter through the ceiling above.

"She . . . er . . . doesn't like cats?" he queried.

6

The volume of the music above became discernibly louder and the suggestion of a cloud began to flicker in and out of the benign expression Gerald tried to keep on his face.

"It's not so much that," Mr Fox explained. "She's allergic to them."

Gerald's lips were still smiling, but as the pop music got louder and louder, his eyes took on a wild, haunted look as they flashed irritably up at the ceiling.

"I see . . . yes . . . that's very distressing!" He spoke with feeling, though at that moment his mind was far from the problems of Mr Fox and his wife's aversion to cats.

"I've been to the police!" the little man went on. "But they don't seem to be able to do anything."

Gerald's reply was lost in the cacophony of sound vibrating down from the floor above.

"What I want to know is . . ." Mr Fox began to shout, ". . . would it be in order for me to put some rat poison down?"

Rat poison! . . . the thought had crossed Gerald's mind more than once in moments of extreme provocation . . . It was an idea, but . . .

"No, no, no, no! That wouldn't do at all!" he exclaimed as he struggled to dismiss the thought from his mind. The alarmed look in his client's eyes brought him back to reality. "You'd lay yourself open to prosecution!" he shouted to make himself heard. "By the RSPCA and the owner!"

"The what and the who?" Mr Fox bellowed back.

"I said . . ." Gerald's voice cracked into a strange falsetto as he tried to top the din from the record player. He looked despairingly at his client, who was looking at the light-fitting swinging on its cord. "Excuse me for a moment!" he bawled. He got up from his desk, tight-faced with fury, straightened himself and strode out through the door, down the corridor and into the hall. As he began to fight his way through the greenery up the stairs, the pop music rose to a deafening, explosive crescendo.

Chapter Two

A Difficult Day

Just as Gerald reached the top of the stairs, the pop music stopped, but the silence didn't reign for long. Almost before the echoes of the last drum beat had died away, it was replaced by the ferocious banging of Gerald's fists on the solid mahogany front door to the Lamperts' flat.

The door opened and the Lamperts' new au pair girl, Adela, stood open-mouthed as Gerald brushed past her and strode furiously into the living-room.

There was no sign of Toby in the room but his three brothers and sister, Joanna, were all there and seemingly indifferent to his fuming presence as he stood glowering at them.

Joanna, a delicate, fey-looking eleven-year-old, smiled sweetly and continued to water the various potted plants scattered around the room, while her twelve-year-old brother, Richard, remained sitting at the dining table where he was studiously experimenting with a pocket calculator.

David, a studious, bespectacled lad of thirteen, was far too engrossed in the offending record-player even to notice the intruder from downstairs. He was standing between two large matching speakers and examining a curious electronic gadget while making notes in an exercise book.

Only the eldest boy, Billy, afforded Gerald as much as a glance. A husky, tough-looking fourteen-year-old, he was vigorously exercising with a pair of dumb-bells when the irate tenant burst in. He greeted him off-handedly, as he continued with his exercises.

"If you've come to apologize to Toby, he's upstairs!"

The insolent expression on the young teenager's face added fuel to the flames of fury already raging in Gerald's breast, and it took a great effort of will for him to remain coherent.

"I am not here to apologize to anyone!" he spat out acidly. "The reason I am . . ."

"Okay, okay!" Bill interrupted. He stopped exercising and stood with the dumb-bells hanging loosely from his arms as he fixed Gerald scornfully. "If you're not big enough to say you're sorry when you're wrong, you could at least get his bike mended!"

Joanna was watering a nearby plant when she was suddenly overcome with compassion for her young brother.

"Yes!" she exclaimed. "Poor Toby!" With the watering-can still in her hand, she turned and looked earnestly up at Gerald. "What's he going to do for the rest of the holidays without his bike?"

"Walk!" he choked, completely unmoved by her appealing eyes. "Preferably to Siberia! Now look . . ."

He broke off, suddenly aware of a presence hovering anxiously behind him. He swung round sharply to behold the bemused face of Adela, looking uncertainly from him to the two children. "Who are you?" he snapped.

"Adela Balinska. The new au pair!"

Bill smirked.

"I see!" Gerald breathed in deeply, exhaling noisily through his nostrils before turning back to address Adela. "Well! Since you are presumably, by dint of your status, in charge of this band of delinquents, would you be so kind as to inform that hooligan over there . . ." he broke off to wag his finger at David, ". . . that, if from my office directly below, I hear one peep from that infernal machine of his, I will return and break it over his head!"

She listened gravely until he had finished speaking, then, as Gerald glared at her, waiting for her reply, a nervous smile flickered across her face.

"Well!" Gerald thundered. "I'm waiting!"

Alarmed by the aggression in his voice, her smile quickly gave way to a look of puzzled bewilderment. She looked appealingly at Bill, who was sniggering to himself.

"Don't hold your breath!" he laughed, tauntingly. "She doesn't understand a word of English!"

Momentarily deflated by Bill's insolent attitude, Gerald snapped, testily.

"Why didn't you say so?"

It was the chance Bill had been waiting for to take another rise out of their unwelcome tenant.

"Because," he said, puffing out his chest in a fair imitation of Gerald at his most pompous, ". . . I thought a person of your considerable intellect would have known that the sole purpose of an au pair coming to England, was to learn English."

Gerald stood and stared, speechless for a moment, then looked across the room and strode over to confront his arch-tormentor, David, who was so engrossed in his calculations that he was, so far, oblivious to the rumpus that had been going on in the room.

"I will endeavour to remain as calm and rational about this as circumstances permit, but . . ." He looked down and stopped suddenly, when he realised that David had not heard a word he'd said. Angrily, he reached out and snatched the notebook from his hand.

David looked round, startled by Gerald's rude interruption, and exclaimed. "What?" As he came round to face Gerald, he was aware of his presence for the first time. Gerald cleared his throat and paused until he had David's full attention. He chose his words carefully and delivered them in a bitingly sarcastic manner.

"I have a client downstairs who may have to be sent to hospital!"

A look of genuine concern came over David's face.

"Why? What's wrong with him?" he asked.

Gerald smiled maliciously and without humour as he repeatedly tapped the record-player.

"Suspected fracturing of the ear-drums!"

"Really?" The surprised look of ill-concealed delight on David's face suggested that for the moment at least, the scientist had gained ascendancy over the humanitarian in him . . . his amplifier must be better than he thought if it had produced the decibels necessary to split ear-drums . . . it had shown no sign of breaking down and was capable of producing far greater volume. He frowned as he looked back to the dials on his equipment . . . they must have been giving out wrong readings or else he'd misread them. He looked up at Gerald and pointed to the meter.

"This is a sound decibel meter!" he explained.

"Really!"

"It measures sound," David went on, quite oblivious to the exasperation in Gerald's voice. "You know . . . how loud something is . . . and I was experimenting to see how much volume it could take before the system broke down."

Gerald's hopes began to rise and there was a sense of relief in his voice.

"And the experiment is now concluded!" he sighed.

David's young brow was furrowed in concentration.

"Not really, no . . ."

Gerald's anger suddenly flared up and he cut in furiously on the young electronic genius.

"Yes, really, yes!" he blazed, thrusting the notebook back into David's hand. Otherwise, we'll be conducting another experiment, together! It will attempt to measure how many times I can clip you round the ear before you break down!"

He turned, sharply, on his heel, straightened himself to his full height and began to stride self-righteously towards the door. As he reached the dining table, he stopped abruptly, his eyes riveted on the object in Richard's hand. Richard smiled up at him, pleasantly.

"Can't seem to work out how you do percentages," he sighed, putting the calculator down on the table.

Gerald picked it up, examined it and looked accusingly at Richard.

"This is mine!"

Richard seemed completely unconcerned by Gerald's accusation and made no attempt to deny that he had taken the calculator.

"Yes!" he said simply. "I borrowed it!"

"Borrowed it!" Gerald raged. "Like you borrowed my camera, cassette-player, stapling machine, typewriter, clock and portable television!"

Richard looked pained.

"You got them all back!"

"I got them back," Gerald snorted, "because I knew whose light, sticky fingers had taken them in the first place!"

Bill put down his dumb-bells and called across the room.

"I don't know what you're making such a fuss about. He didn't break any of them or anything!"

"That's hardly the point!" Gerald retorted, turning round sharply to face Bill. "Borrowing is when you ask permission!"

"You were probably out."

The insolent grin on Bill's face was like a red rag to a bull.

"Of course I was out!" Gerald stormed. "If I'd been in, he wouldn't have got through the door!" As Bill shrugged his shoulders and turned away, Gerald grabbed his arm and swung him round to bring him face to face. "Get this into your brother's thick head, that the police have a word for borrowing without permission. It's called stealing! And if he does it once more, they'll be explaining that to him personally!"

He looked round with a wild, desperate look in his eyes . . . how could one impress anything on this family? Richard was still sitting at the table, smiling to himself, while David was poring over his notes and making adjustments to his equipment. As for Joanna, she'd opted out of the fray completely and was back in her own world, rearranging the greenery in the room. For all the impression Gerald had made, he might as well have talked to a brick wall. Exhausted, he summoned up the strength for one last, withering look at Bill, threw up his hands and turned to make for the door.

Just at that moment, Toby came into the room from upstairs.

"I'm going to take my bike round to the shop to get it mended," he said, adding pointedly to Gerald. "I shall tell them to send you the bill!"

"And I shall send it straight back!" Gerald hissed. He was beginning to feel faint and clutched his head as he turned and charged, straight into the outstretched arm of Adela, who was standing in the doorway. He stared, blank-faced, as she flicked through the pages of a small pocket dictionary. Suddenly her face lit up as she found what she was looking for.

"Good day!" she beamed.

"Not so far!" he muttered through his teeth.

Back in Gerald's office, Mr Fox tutted in vexation as he looked at his watch for the umpteenth time. It really was too bad of Mr Parish to leave him like this . . . most unprofessional . . . and bad-mannered, come to that! Through the half-open door to the outer office, he could hear the monotonous clicking of Miss Wright's knitting needles, and that irritated him beyond measure . . . not that he'd anything against knitting, but there was a time and place for everything . . . and the right time was certainly not during business hours and a solicitor's office was most definitely not the right place. The very idea!

Suddenly he heard the door to the outer office burst open, and Gerald came charging through.

"Mr Fox, my humblest apologies!" he boomed in a tone that was far from humble. "As you see, I am plagued by a family of maniacs upstairs!" He crossed to behind his desk, sat down and began to address himself to his client's problem. "Now, where were we? Ah, yes . . . the cat! We were not going to poison the cat . . . no need! There's a very simple solution to your problem, Mr Fox!" He beamed superficially across the desk as his client edged himself forward in anticipation. "Buy a dog!"

Mr Fox recoiled, as though he'd been shot.

"Oh no! . . . I couldn't possibly do that!"

Gerald frowned with annoyance.

"Why not?" he demanded.

13

"I don't like dogs!"

Gerald's patience was at a low ebb.

"Mr Fox!" He cleared his throat and tried to dispel all thoughts of the family upstairs from his mind, but try as he did, he couldn't prevent his antagonism towards them spilling over into his cultivated, professional manner. "You came to me with a problem and I, in my humble opinion, have solved it in the simplest, most economical and the most practical way. Now if you . . ."

He broke off suddenly, as the door burst open and Mary Lampert strode into the room. She was an attractive woman in her late thirties, and particularly so when inflamed with anger. Gerald leapt up from his seat and fumed.

"How dare you just burst into my office! This is private property!"

"So is my flat upstairs!" she shouted angrily, as she advanced towards him. "But that didn't stop you, did it?"

Mr Fox sat, transfixed, as the tempest raged around him.

"I had just cause!" Gerald choked furiously. "First of all, one of your children was playing that infernal record player loud enough to wake the dead and secondly I discovered that your kleptomaniac son had stolen this!" He waved the calculator excitedly under her nose.

She brushed it aside, laughing mockingly.

"Aaaah. Did he take your calculator away from you, did he? Never mind! Mummy will buy you another one!"

"Don't you be facetious with me!" Gerald blazed. "That boy is a thief!"

Mary suddenly froze inside and her expression became serious.

"How many times do I have to tell you, Richard is ill!" She spoke earnestly, looking directly into Gerald's eyes, almost pleading with him to believe her. "He doesn't know it's wrong to borrow things . . ."

"Steal things!" Gerald corrected her.

"All right!" she flared up defiantly. "But he will be cured!" She spoke with great emphasis but her words lacked conviction. "It takes time and patience . . ." she looked up at Gerald, but his expression was far from sympathetic, "and it doesn't help to have people like you shouting at him and threatening him with the police!" she shouted accusingly.

"You should send him away somewhere," Gerald suggested blandly. "To a home of some sort!"

"He's got a home! Here!" Mary cried, fighting back the fears that were always there when she thought of Richard. "He has to lead a normal life if we're going to break him of this . . . this habit and . . . and . . . while we're on the subject of breakages, I get back to the house to find that . . ."

Gerald anticipated what was coming and stepped in quickly.

"I'm not paying to mend that damned bike!" he shouted.

Mr Fox decided that he had had enough of Mr Parish's professional services and as the antagonists continued to slang each other, got up nervously from his chair, and sidled, unnoticed, out through the door.

"It was your foot that went through Toby's wheels!" Mary stormed.

"And Toby's wheels were parked illegally and dangerously inside the front door!" Gerald retorted, going on pompously to say. "Now, if you'd like me to show you the lease, I can assure you . . ."

She was quick to reject his offer, cutting in on him before he'd finished speaking.

"No thank you!" she cried. "I know it by heart. I read it through every night, just in case I've missed a little clause somewhere, which would entitle me to throw you out of here."

"Don't waste your time!" he laughed, smugly. "There isn't one!" It was his first taste of victory in what had been a disastrous day, and he sought to press home his advantage by shepherding his dejected adversary out of his office. "And now if you'll excuse me!" he beamed magnanimously, waving his arm towards the door as he

15

turned to go back to his desk. Suddenly, he stopped dead in his tracks as his eyes fell on the vacant chair on the other side of the desk and he noticed for the first time that Mr Fox was no longer in the office. He swung round angrily on Mary.

"Brilliant!" he hissed. "Between you and that lunatic, deranged family of yours, you have lost me the best client I've had this week!"

"Well, that's some compensation!" she snapped, as she swept out through the door.

He glared after her and suddenly, in a fit of sheer frustration, aimed a ferocious kick at the waste-paper basket. It sailed into the air, skidded over the desk and scattered its contents all over the floor.

Miss Wright, in the outer office, alarmed by the extraordinary happenings of the morning, rushed to the doorway just in time to see her principal slump dejectedly, head in hands, across the desk.

Chapter Three

Out of the Blue

Next morning, Gerald was up with the lark, determined to erase the memory of that fearful day completely from his mind. The dining table in his flat was most beautifully laid out for breakfast and through the louvred doors, in the kitchen, wearing a chef's hooped apron over his pyjamas, Gerald was putting the finishing touches to a kedgeree which would have delighted the palate of the most fastidious gourmet — which indeed he was. He was humming happily to himself as he pushed open the swing doors with his shoulder and bore the silver entrée dish containing his creation to the table. He took off his apron, folded it carefully and put it neatly in the drawer of the sideboard, before sitting down at the table and rubbing his hands in anticipation of his culinary masterpiece.

He smiled smugly to himself . . . considering the scant number of clients on his books, Gerald Parish, Solicitor and Commissioner for Oaths enjoyed quite a remarkable life-style . . . Quite remarkable! It it weren't for the aggravation from the family upstairs, life would be . . . but then again, he mused, 'It's an ill wind that . . .' He uncovered the entrée dish, and sat for a moment with eyes half closed, breathing in the delicate, mouth-watering aroma of his gourmet breakfast.

"Exquisite!" he murmured, opening his eyes and taking the first forkful of the kedgeree to his mouth. He was just beginning to savour the first, delicious mouthful when the telephone began to ring. He grimaced with annoyance, took a sip of coffee and got up to answer it. He snatched up the receiver and snapped curtly into the mouthpiece.

"Yes?"

"Mr Gerald Parish?" the operator crooned. "Hold the line please! I have a long-distance call for you."

A frown creased Gerald's brow as he waited for the mysterious caller to be connected. Who on earth could it be, ringing at this time in the morning . . . It was unlikely to be a friend and if it was a client, why the devil couldn't he ring after breakfast . . . during office hours? . . . Long distance . . . he didn't have any long-distance clients!

"Gerald?"

The aggressive, masculine voice had a familiar ring, but Gerald couldn't quite place it among any of his clients . . . it was all very perplexing.

"Yes! Who's that?"

The voice at the other end of the line showed signs of irritation.

"Henry Parish!"

Gerald was getting confused, and it showed as he stammered into the mouthpiece.

"Yes, this is Mr Parish! Who is that speaking?"

"Your father, you idiot!" the voice roared.

The receiver almost fell from Gerald's hand as the shock waves vibrated through his body . . . he had not seen his father for years . . . not since he had retired as a High Court judge and opted for the sunshine of the Bahamas.

"My fa . . . er . . . You . . . ?"

"My God, you haven't changed, have you?" the old judge boomed down the line. "Fifteen years since I last spoke to you and you're still stuttering and gibbering like an embarrassed schoolgirl!"

Gerald winced and held the receiver away from his ear . . . the old man hadn't changed either! . . . still the same old endearing father . . . My God! He made a great effort to pull himself together.

"I'm sorry, I er . . . Well, how are you, father?"

"Let's dispense with the formalities, shall we, Gerald? You don't care a damn how I am and I care even less about how you are! So just get a pencil and paper and write down what I tell you!''

Gerald quickly got a pencil and notepad and returned to the phone.

''Right! Pencil and paper at the ready, sir!''

He took down the message as the old man dictated it.

''British Airways Flight 217 . . . Arrival time sixteen hundred hours . . . Tuesday . . . the twenty-fifth of this month. Got it?''

''. . . the twenty-fifth, yes I've got that.''

''Right! Then you will have a car waiting at the airport to take me to my hotel!'' he commanded.

There was undisguised horror in Gerald's voice as he stammered into the phone.

''You're coming over? Over here?''

There was an exasperated snort from the other side of the world.

''I should have thought that was painfully obvious by now!''

Gerald swallowed hard as he tried to sound pleased.

''Well . . . How marvellous, I mean I . . .''

The old judge was not fooled and cut straight across him.

''Just have a car there to meet me!''

''I shall be there personally to meet you, sir!'' Gerald fawned.

''Don't bother! It's not you I'm coming to see! I'm coming to see my grandchildren!''

Gerald gulped, but before he could say anything, the receiver slammed down on its rest, four thousand miles away. He was completely shattered and for some moments just stared vacantly at the phone in his hand. Then, still in a trance, he put down the receiver and staggered over to the dining table.

''The twenty-fifth!'' he groaned. ''That's a week on Friday.''

Absent-mindedly, he picked up a fork and started to eat his breakfast. The kedgeree was cold and tasted like sawdust. He pushed the food away from him and auto-

19

matically reached for the cup to wash the taste from his mouth with cold coffee. He grimaced and put the cup down.

Suddenly a look of alarm came over his face.

"His grandchildren!" he exclaimed. He sighed wearily, and groaned. "Oh my God!"

"Adela, finish laying the table, will you?"

Mary saw the blank look on the Polish girl's face and proceeded to mime the action of laying the table as she repeated her instructions, slowly and distinctly.

"Lay . . . the . . . table!"

"Aaaah!" The au pair's eyes lit up as the message became clear to her, and she at once began to lay seven places at the table while Mary went back to the kitchen to finish preparing the breakfast.

Moments later, Mary reappeared from the kitchen with the toast, put it down on the table next to the cereals and marmalade, glanced around quickly to check that everything was ready, and went to the foot of the stairs to give the signal for battle to commence.

"Children! Breakfast!"

Almost before the words were out of her mouth, the commotion began, with children, dressing-gowns hastily thrown over their pyjamas, cascading, sliding, tumbling downstairs in the mad rush to the table. The noise was deafening and though Mary was used to it, she still covered her ears until the squabbling had died down before joining them at the table. For the new au pair girl, unaccustomed to the shouts of 'Shove up!', 'Keep your elbows in', 'How much room do you want?' etc., it was an utterly bewildering experience.

They had just about finished breakfast, and Mary was helping them to their second cups of coffee, when there was a knock at the front door. Adela was happy to have an excuse to go and practice her limited vocabulary.

"Good day!" she said brightly as she opened the door. She started apprehensively when she saw Gerald standing in the doorway and remembered the shouting match of the day before, but she need not have worried. The man from downstairs was, it seemed, a totally transformed character. He beamed at her as he responded to her greeting.

"One hopes!" he smiled, peering past her and waving to the family around the table. "Very, very sorry to interrupt you while you're having your breakfast!"

There was a complete silence from Mary and the children as they stared at each other in utter disbelief.

"The thing is . . ." he called over from the door. ". . . Well I had occasion to venture out quite early this morning and on my way back, I happened to pass the bicycle shop." He moved, a little uncertainly, towards the table and addressed himself to Toby. "Since your bicycle happened to be repaired, I thought I'd save you the trouble of collecting it yourself . . . and . . . well, it's downstairs!"

Toby was nothing if not direct . . . he wouldn't have minded collecting the bike himself . . . there were, in his mind, more important considerations.

"What about paying for it?" he asked, flatly.

"Done! All taken care of!" Gerald waved his hand in an expansive gesture. "Yes," he smiled, "on reflection, I felt that it was perhaps my responsibility and . . . Oh! You may notice I've had a new bell fitted, also at my expense. The old one seemed to be a little rusty!"

The family were quite convinced they were dreaming. They all exchanged looks with each other and then turned to stare unbelievingly at Gerald. It was some moments before Mary broke the silence.

"Thank you very much, Mr Parish!"

"My pleasure!" he beamed, and after a short pause, turned towards the door. "Well, I won't intrude any longer . . ."

"Have a good day!" he chirped brightly as he went out through the door.

As the door closed behind him, the family just sat and stared in stunned silence. They had all heard of dramatic conversions, but even in 'The Lives of the Saints' it would have been hard to find records of a conversion

21

more dramatic than the one they had, apparently, just witnessed.

"Heavens! I shall be late for the office!" Mary gasped as she came out of her trance. "Where's my handbag?" She pushed her way past her gaping children, grabbed her handbag and rushed out through the door.

Chapter Four

The Last Straw

It was fortunate that Gerald had no appointments that day for he was clearly out of sorts. Nesta was so concerned about his condition that she put down her knitting long enough to make him a pot of hot black coffee. This did much to restore his calm but he still felt exhausted and needed little urging by his ever attentive Nesta to take the rest of the day off and put his feet up.

He took a light lunch of smoked salmon followed by cold chicken and honey-roasted Wiltshire ham accompanied by tossed salad and finished off with a modest cheeseboard of Blue Stilton, Gorgonzola and Windsor Red. His appetite was impaired by his overwrought condition and he couldn't face a sweet, just black coffee and a large brandy which he took to his bedroom and sipped as he lay under the duvet.

Before closing his eyes, he remembered to set the alarm clock to go off at half past six — just half an hour before his favourite TV programme was due to start.

Thus prepared, he drained the last drop of brandy from the glass, put his head on the pillow and was soon well away from the cares and frustrations of the family upstairs.

Meanwhile, upstairs in the Lampert's kitchen, David was standing in front of the main fuse box, completing the installation of a complicated-looking gadget which he had wired into the incoming 'mains' electricity supply. The job completed, he stood back to admire his handiwork and then turned to explain the complexity of the operation to a bored-looking Toby who was standing watching him.

23

"This," he said, pointing to the gadget with his insulated screwdriver, "is a 'rheostat'. Now I'll explain what that does."

"I know what it does," Toby answered sullenly.

David turned and smiled down his nose at Toby. It was the patronising smile of the thirteen-year-old genius looking down on his seven-year-old kid brother.

"Okay 'Clever Boy'!" he humoured him. "What does it do?"

Toby replied without a moment's hesitation.

"It's a variable resistance that when applied to incoming amperage of an electricity supply will alter the level of reception from that supply."

David gaped with astonishment as he listened to the text-book answer come, parrot-fashion, from the mouth of his young brother, and for a moment felt that his position as the family 'genius' was being challenged. It was just not possible that a mere seven-year-old could understand the complexities of advanced electronics. It just wasn't possible. He must have read it somewhere. He looked down at Toby, who seemed amused by his older brother's bewildered expression.

"Science for Beginners?" he suggested anxiously. His confidence began to return when Toby nodded his head in the affirmative. "You don't know what it all means, do you?"

Toby grinned sheepishly and shook his head.

"Nope," he replied.

David breathed a sigh of relief and the superior smile returned to his face as he took his screwdriver and made the final adjustments to the equipment.

The knife was poised in his hand, and he was about to cut into the Châteaubriand as the alarm bell went off in his ear. His hand reached out, automatically, from under the covers and switched it off. Slowly, the vision faded and he turned onto his back, stretched, yawned, sat up in bed and blinked around at the familiar objects in the room.

24

Sleep is a great healer and Gerald had slept well. Hours of unbroken sleep, disturbed only by visions of exotic places and gastronomic delights. He felt refreshed and the aggravations of the family upstairs had receded into the background of his consciousness — like a half-remembered bad dream that never really happened.

He glanced at the clock on the bedside table. There was just half an hour before his programme began — just time to freshen up — a quick shower and a light snack from the fridge before settling down with his pencil and notebook in front of the television.

The news was just ending when he switched on the set and settled himself comfortably in front of it, notebook in hand and pencil at the ready.

"And now, 'Cordon Bleu for the Gourmet'," came the announcement and as the female presenter came onto the screen, Gerald reached forward and turned up the volume so that he wouldn't miss a word of the exotic recipe she was demonstrating. His mouth watered as she described the superb gourmet casserole and he scribbled furiously as she went on to demonstrate the preparation.

". . . and after the celery has been thoroughly washed and trimmed, it must be plunged into boiling water and allowed to boil for exactly nine minutes . . ."

The suggestion of a frown crossed Gerald's brow. There seemed to be something wrong with his eyes, for he had difficulty in reading the notes as he wrote them. Or else it was the light. He looked momentarily away from the screen and glanced up at the light bulb — it was alight alright, but didn't seem to be shining with anything like its usual brilliance. When he looked back at the screen, there seemed to be something wrong there too. It seemed smaller, and he had to lean forward in his chair to watch the final part of the demonstration.

". . . and now the truffles have, repeat have to be put into the casserole at exactly the right time. So we have the veal and the herbs and the diced anchovies, now the . . ."

Up above, in the Lampert's kitchen, David was giving a

different kind of demonstration to his young brother. Having listened reluctantly to David's boring technical exposition of his modification to the electricity supply, Toby was all agog now that the talking had stopped and it really seemed that something was actually about to happen.

"Now you see," David explained with his hand on the control knob. "As I turn down the resistance . . ."

Toby watched with amazement as the lights in the room noticeably dimmed before his eyes; ". . . so the power drops as the supply is reduced."

David started momentarily as he heard his mother's voice calling through from the living room.

"Who's messing about with the lights? David!"

"Won't be a sec," David called back, crossing over to close the kitchen door before going back to continue the demonstration.

"Now if we take it all the way down . . ."

His hand was on the control knob as the door burst open and his mother came into the room.

"All right, now that's enough!" she commanded. "David, disconnect that thing at once and Toby! Five minutes to bedtime."

Meanwhile, down below in his flat, Gerald was having great difficulty as he tried to get down the final cooking instructions for the veal casserole. The television picture had got smaller and smaller until it became no larger than a postage stamp, and he was kneeling in front of the set in a vain attempt to see the end of the demonstration.

". . . and now we come to the final ingredient and this is where so many people go wrong . . ."

Gerald's nose was almost touching the screen, and he was still trying to take notes in what was almost total darkness.

The presenter's voice went on.

". . . you must, and I cannot emphasise this enough, you must, at this point add the so essential half pint of . . ."

26

Suddenly the sound and picture went completely dead and Gerald exploded in a fit of absolute frustration. He shook his fist and glared through the blackness to the ceiling above, screaming distractedly.

"That bloody tin-pot Edison!"

He was still on his knees when the lights and television came back on. The picture was back to its normal size and the presenter was beaming at him from the screen.

"Well, that's it for this week," she purred. "And next week, Cordon Bleu for the Gourmet will tackle . . ."

Gerald snapped the set off in disgust and staggered to his feet. He stood, fuming, for a moment. Then he looked down at the notebook in his hand and flung it across the room, and in a fit of blind, uncontrolled fury, stormed over to the door, tore it open and shouted hysterically out into the hall.

"That's it! I've had enough! I can't stand it any more! I hate the lot of you! I hate and loathe you! Do you hear!" He was quite oblivious to the telephone ringing in his flat as he ranted on. "I hate, loathe and despise you!"

The persistent ringing of the phone eventually registered on his mind and he strode back into the room, grabbed the receiver and snapped into the mouthpiece.

"Hold on!" He slammed the receiver down on its rest and charged back to the doorway. "I'm going mad. You know that? You're driving me mad!"

There was no response from upstairs and he stepped out into the hall and bawled up the stairs.

"Do you hear me! You come ranting and raving into my office and lose me all my clients!" The telephone was ringing again in his flat. He strode back into the room and tore the receiver from its rest.

"I said hold on!" he snarled, putting the handset down on the table and rushing back to the door. "That pint-sized kleptomaniac 'borrows' all my possessions, and now I can't even watch the television in peace! He tore out into the hall and shouted up the stairs. "I don't care about the consequences! Do you hear me? I don't care any more!" He paused for breath and suddenly remembered the telephone was off its hook. He strode back into the room and lifted the receiver.

"Yes!" he snapped.

Thousands of miles away, at the other end of the line, Judge Henry Parish was getting impatient. For several minutes he had been paying for a transatlantic call for the dubious privilege of hearing his son having a shouting match with himself.

"Feeling better now, are we?" he replied, acidly.

Gerald took a deep breath and tried to compose himself.

"Oh yes . . . Hello sir . . ." he stammered as he tried to get a firmer grip on himself. "Slight problem with the neighbours. All sorted out now."

His father dismissed his explanation with a grunt and got straight down to the nitty gritty.

"Some idiot in the travel agency gave me the wrong information. Same flight number, same time only it's the twenty-fourth. I'll be arriving a week on Thursday! Got it?"

"Right. Yes," Gerald replied with forced enthusiasm. "Can't wait to see you, sir."

Henry Parish was not a very patient man and it required a considerable effort of will to force patience into his voice.

"Gerald!" he barked. "I think it might be as well we understand each other very clearly as of now . . ." The old man was looking at two silver-framed photographs which were standing on his desk. They were both recent ones of Mary and the children. "It's not you I'm coming over to see. In fact, I really wouldn't mind if you weren't there. So why don't you take a short holiday? I am coming over to see your wife and meet my grandchildren. Is that quite clear?" There was nothing ambiguous in what the old judge had said but he was leaving nothing to chance. Any lingering doubt that might have persisted in Gerald's mind was dispelled when the old man reiterated. "The only reason I'm coming over is to see my grandchildren. Got it?"

"Got it," Gerald echoed, weakly. "Right. Well er . . . yes . . ." he was beginning to feel punch drunk from the battering he had received from all sides. "The . . . er car will be at the er . . ."

"What?"

The old man's bark brought him up sharp as it had done when he was a child, for neither advancing years nor the thousands of miles of transatlantic cable, did anything to diminish the ferocity of the old judge's voice. Gerald gulped and pulled himself together.

"The car will be at the airport to meet you, sir."

"That's better!" Henry grunted. "Anyway, think about that holiday idea!" He slammed down the receiver, leaving Gerald staring vacantly into the mouthpiece at the other end. Slowly, he replaced the phone on its rest.

"You all right, Mr Parish?"

He swung round to see Toby standing anxiously in the doorway, wearing a dressing gown over his pyjamas. The boy looked concerned.

"You're not ill, are you Mr Parish? We heard a lot of shouting and Mummy said to come down and see if you were okay."

Gerald smiled back weakly and managed to find his voice.

"No. I'm fine, Toby. Fine, thank you."

A look of relief spread over Toby's face.

"Oh good! Well . . . Goodnight then, Mr Parish!"

He turned and went out of the room, closing the door behind him. Gerald just sat and stared at the closed door. He felt numb, drained of feeling. Suddenly he put his hand to his head and cried out.

"Oh my God!"

It was a despairing cry that came straight from the heart.

Chapter Five

The Challenge

Mary had little time to listen to the complaints of her children as she bustled around, trying to sort out the shambles in the living-room. She had to leave for the office in a few minutes and it was a little trying to have four of them trailing after her wherever she moved.

"David won't let me play my record on his hi-fi!" Toby whined.

"'Cause last time he broke it. That's why!" David moaned, defensively.

"Then you play it and Toby can listen to it," she advised with all the patience she could muster, before turning to face them and pointing to the records lying all over the floor. "And I want all those records picked up and put away in their proper place . . ." She broke off suddenly as her eyes lit upon a little terrier, lying curled up in an armchair. "That's a dog!" she gasped.

"Right!" David confirmed.

"But we don't have a dog!" She looked questioningly at the children for an explanation, but none was forth-coming.

Richard was shuffling around uneasily.

"Richard!"

He turned round to face his mother but avoided meeting her eyes as he muttered, defensively, "I borrowed it."

"Then you'd better unborrow it!" she flared. "Or better still, return it to its owner." She examined the dog's collar and read out the address. "22 Larchborough Road might be a good place to start." She turned to Joanna, waving her hand in the direction of some toys which were scattered all over the floor. "Joanna! I want all those toys put back neatly in your bedroom.''

Joanna tried to take the heat off with a diversionary tactic.

"Adela broke the big pudding basin."

Mary gave a short sigh and raised her eyes.

"Oh dear! Well, never mind." She turned back to Joanna. "Now Joanna! I meant it about those toys, otherwise they go straight into the dustbin." She turned round sharply just as David was making 'hard luck' signs to Joanna. "Oh, David! Did you tidy your room like I asked? It looked like it'd been hit by a hurricane."

"All done," he answered, a little too glibly.

Mary moved quickly towards the stairs.

"I'll just go and check . . ."

David broke in on her, "Except for a few bits and pieces. I'll do it later."

Mary turned back from the stairs and looked him severely in the eye.

"You'd better!" She moved off towards the kitchen just as a crestfallen Adela was coming into the room.

"Don't worry about the pudding basin, Adela. Accidents can happen," she called.

Adela was struggling with her phrase-book.

"The big pudding basin . . ." She looked up, but Mary had already gone past her into the kitchen, ". . . which Joanna is . . ."

Joanna moved across and touched her on the arm.

"It's all right, Adela. I've explained to Mummy," she tried to reassure her.

As the bewildered au pair gazed uncomprehendingly at Joanna, David moved over and gave her the thumbs-up sign.

"It's OK about the basin, Adela."

She understood David's gesture and, smiling gratefully, nodded her head.

Mary was still on the rampage as she came storming in from the kitchen.

"That kitchen looks like Bill's been having a fight with the Incredible Hulk," she exclaimed. "By the way,

31

where is Bill?''

There was a silence as the children anxiously exchanged glances. They all knew what Bill had been up to but they weren't going to split on him. It was Toby who eventually broke the silence.

''He went out. He hasn't come back yet.''

The other three children nodded their agreement, but their mother wasn't fooled for a moment and was already moving over to the bottom of the stairs.

''Bill!'' she yelled. ''Come down here this minute!'' She turned back to the children. ''I suppose he's been fighting again?''

She'd hit the nail right on the head and Richard, sensing trouble for Bill, stepped in and desperately tried to pour oil on the troubled waters.

''Oh I remember now!'' he lied. ''Bill went out to play football and . . .''

''And he did come back home 'cause somebody kicked the ball right in his face . . .'' David chipped in, eagerly compounding Richard's perjury. ''Didn't want to mention it in case it upset you.''

''Poor Bill!'' Joanna sighed, dramatically.

''It's right, mum!'' Toby added, not to be outdone. ''You should have seen his eye!''

''I'm looking at it!'' She was looking up the stairs as Bill came down sporting a king-size 'shiner'. As he came into the room, she shook her head sadly and sighed. ''Well! Who was it this time?''

''John Jenkins,'' Bill replied, sheepishly. ''He called me a poof.''

Bill was always getting into fights, and nothing Mary said to him seemed to make any difference. The boy just wouldn't listen to reason.

''So you hit him and he hit you,'' she said, looking at him earnestly. ''Now what did that achieve?''

Bill shrugged his shoulders and pointed to his black eye.

''This, I suppose,'' he grimaced.

''And what about the other boy, John er . . . whatever his name is?''

Bill grinned painfully.

"Not a pretty sight."

Mary threw up her hands in despair.

"There's some ointment in the bathroom cabinet," she sighed. "You'd better put some on that eye." She looked at her watch, hastily grabbed her handbag from the table and made for the door, turning in the doorway to give her last instructions before dashing out to the office. "Now do make Adela understand that I'll be late home tonight!"

"Why?" Toby asked.

"Because she'll have to feed you and tuck you in," she smiled.

"I didn't mean that," Toby persisted. "I mean why will you be late?"

Children could be so difficult sometimes and it made any kind of social life almost impossible — every time she didn't come straight home from the office, there was always the endless interrogation. She looked at the concerned expressions on the children's faces — Perhaps it was understandable. She smiled patiently.

"I'm going out with Mr Purvis."

Bill glowered belligerently.

"You went out with him last night."

Her eldest boy's attitude put her on the defensive and the only form of defence she knew was attack.

"Well, I'm going out with him again tonight!" she bristled, defiantly. She paused for a moment in the doorway to gather her wits. Then she smiled and blew kisses to each of the five children. "Be good! If that's possible."

They watched, solemn-faced, as the door closed behind their mother. As they exchanged glances with each other, they each knew what the others were thinking. They felt somehow less secure, threatened by the stranger in their mother's life. It was Joanna who finally broke the silence.

"Will we still be called Lampert if Mummy marries again?" she asked.

As Mary rushed out through the gate, she almost bumped

into Gerald, who was on his way back to the house, carrying an enormous rectangular package. She bade him a brisk 'Good Morning' but by the time he had recovered his balance enough to respond, she was already half-way across the Square.

He staggered up to the front door, pushed it open with his bottom and started to back in. Remembering previous painful encounters with Toby's bicycle, he reached out gingerly with his foot and located the bike so as to avoid it when he stepped, backwards, into the hall. He was completely unaware of the roller skates lying on the hall floor, directly in his path, and it was little short of a miracle that his foot didn't land on them. He turned round in the hall and made his way to his office, blissfully ignorant of the danger he had escaped by a whisker.

As he entered the outer office, Nesta was, as usual, knitting away happily, not even pausing as she looked at the complicated-looking pattern lying on the desk at her side. She looked up to see Gerald struggling with his package as he closed the door behind him.

"Did anyone telephone while I was out, Nesta?" Gerald gasped, resting his package on the desk while wiping his brow.

"No," said Nesta, as her needles continued to click away.

He went through to his own office and began to unwrap the parcel. Nesta was peering over his shoulder as he took off the brown paper wrapping and could see that it was a large, framed portrait of a gentleman in Judge's robes. Ignoring her gasps of appreciation, Gerald took the portrait and proceeded to hang it on the wall. When he had positioned it to his liking, he turned to Nesta.

"Better give it a bit of a dusting, Nesta," he grunted, "in case the old goat calls round when he's over here."

"Oh, really, Mr Parish," she reproved him. "You shouldn't say things like that about your own father!"

He laughed and crossed back to the desk.

"Only behind his back, Nesta." He sat at the desk and smiled, hypocritically up at her. "Never to his face!"

She gave a little shocked exclamation that fell some-where between a huff and a squeak, tossed her head in the air, and trotted back to her own office.

Gerald grinned as he watched her go off in high dudgeon, and then turned back to concentrate on a list of figures on his desk. He studied the list for a few moments and then reached out automatically to the position where his calculator should have been. As his hands clutched only the air above the polished surface, his eyes flashed to the empty space on the desk in front of him. He immediately froze and clenching his teeth, rose unsteadily from his chair.

"That little thief's been in here again!" he spluttered, his eyes blazing with fury. He breathed in deeply, pulled himself up to his full height and charged out of his office, past the bewildered Nesta into the hall, and bounded the greenery-strewn stairs three at a time to the flat above.

A startled Adela opened the door to his frenzied pound-ing and was positively terrified when he spat out belligerently:

"Calculator!"

"Calcol. . ." she gasped open-mouthed as he brushed past her and advanced towards the children.

"When I say calculator," he fumed, "I'm in effect saying Richard."

Adela, coming in behind him, was quite bewildered by what she thought she'd heard him say and thumbed frantically through her phrase book to find confirmation. The children were equally puzzled by the sudden change of attitude in the man downstairs. Bill looked up at him from the sofa.

"Well, Richard's not here at the moment. He's taking the dog for a walk."

Gerald bristled at the mention of a dog. He had cun-ningly inserted a clause in the lease against either party keeping pets, and this was a direct breach of the agree-ment.

"If Richard has a dog, I should have been informed about it," he snapped.

"Richard hasn't got a dog," Bill interjected.

Gerald swung round triumphantly, in his best courtroom manner.

"Then whose dog is he taking for a walk, pray?"

"It's a dog he . . ." Bill was beginning to feel a bit uncomfortable and looked around to the others for support. They all looked on in silence as he sighed and continued, ". . . it's a dog he . . . borrowed."

"I see!" Gerald pounced. "Like he 'borrows' everything else he takes a fancy to. Like he's borrowed my calculator for the third time this week." He snapped his fingers impatiently at the children. "I have important business being held up." He shot his open hand under Bill's nose, "Calculator. Now!" he demanded.

There was a pause as Bill, David and Toby looked helplessly from one to the other. Then Joanna got up, moved over to one of her bushier plants, extracted the calculator from under the foliage and handed it timidly to Gerald. He snatched it from her hand.

"Thank you very much for returning my own property!" he said sarcastically. "So very good of you to return it!"

He glared round at each of the children in turn, turned on his heel and strode out past the confused au pair, who was still trying to catch up on the proceedings with the help of her dictionary.

"Calcolat . . . calccolit . . ." she muttered, as she laboriously scanned the pages. The door slamming behind Gerald almost caused her to jump out of her skin. At this point she gave up the ghost, snapping the dictionary shut and ambling disconsolately into the kitchen to finish the washing up.

The children were still bemused by the mercurial change in Gerald from the previous day and they looked questioningly from one to the other.

"It's funny," David said, thoughtfully, "but I thought he'd changed. You know . . . for the better! Become more friendly!"

Bill was more cynical. He'd never really believed in Gerald's conversion anyhow, and in his mind, the performance they'd just witnessed was Gerald reverting to type.

"Change?" he laughed, sneeringly. "Not him! Turn a leopard inside out and the spots'll still show through!"

Nesta put down her knitting and half rose from her chair as Gerald stormed in, clutching the calculator in his hand. There was a scowl on his face, but he didn't seem to notice her as he charged through the outer office to his room. She peered anxiously round the door and was amazed to see him glaring up at his father's portrait. Then, suddenly, he put his hand to his head and cried out.

"What am I doing?"

Nesta was quite alarmed by her boss's strange behaviour and called out anxiously:

"Sorry, Mr Parish. Did you say something?"

He clearly didn't hear her and continued to stare up at the portrait.

"I must be mad! Stark, raving mad!" he cried.

In all the time she had worked for him, Nesta had never seen him in such a strange mood. She crept over to the doorway and stood, watching with nervous apprehension as he addressed the portrait on the wall.

"Eight days and I have to provide you with a family!"

By now, Nesta was quite confused and not a little concerned for her employer's sanity. Perhaps he was having a nervous breakdown and maybe she should call the doctor. She coughed nervously and called out:

"Mr Parish!"

He swung round sharply to face her.

"Is there something I can do?"

"Yes!"

She backed away, nervously, as he advanced towards her into the outer office.

"Go out and buy another calculator!" he said, moving past her to the entrance door. "Take the money out of the petty cash!"

He was still clutching the calculator as he disappeared through the door into the hall, and Nesta was more bemused than ever by his strange request. She stared after him unbelievingly for a moment, then shook her head resignedly and tutting and fretting to herself, took the keys to the safe and prepared to do his bidding.

The children were all busily engaged in their own pursuits when a knock came on the door. Bill glanced up from the book he was reading and looked hopefully to the others to answer the door. When none of them responded, he threw down his book, yawned, and staggered up from the sofa. He was half-way to the door when he was overtaken by Adela, who had come rushing in from the kitchen. As she opened the door, Gerald smiled at her, walked straight into the room and advanced towards the children.

"Ah! Richard!" he exclaimed as he spotted his face behind an array of Joanna's potted plants.

As Richard emerged hesitantly into the clearing, he spotted the calculator in Gerald's hand.

"I only borrowed it . . ." he stammered, defensively.

Gerald moved close to him and put his hand on his shoulder.

"Of course you did, Richard," he said, soothingly. "No problem! No harm done!"

The other children stared at each other in utter amazement, confused by Gerald's constantly changing moods. They just couldn't believe their eyes when they saw Gerald hand the calculator to Richard.

"To save you the trouble of going up and down stairs in the future," he beamed, "I'm making a present of it to you."

There was a stunned silence for some moments before a bewildered Richard finally exclaimed:

"Thank you, Mr Parish!"

"My pleasure Richard!" Gerald smiled broadly. "My pleasure!"

He turned towards the door and stopped abruptly as he beheld a heavy, thick-set man standing in the doorway.

Only Bill seemed to recognise the intruder and tried to make himself inconspicuous by going back to the sofa and burying his head in his book.

The stranger glared belligerently at Gerald.

"All right! Which one of your kids beat up my son?"

Gerald was quite taken aback by the man's offensive attitude and stammered, confusedly:

"These are, er . . . these are not actually my children. I'm afraid you must have got the wrong house."

The man's lip curled unpleasantly as he pushed his way past Gerald and glared at each of the boys in turn.

"Somehow I don't think so!" he snarled, triumphantly, pointing accusingly at Bill. "It was you, wasn't it?"

Bill coloured guiltily as the irate Ron Jenkins went on.

"Right! Now what you need is a good thrashing and that's just what I'm going to . . ."

He stopped in his tracks as Gerald stepped between them and put out a restraining arm.

"I should warn you that I am a Solicitor at Law," he began loftily, "and if you wish to avoid prosecution for trespass, maximum penalty five hundred pounds, I suggest you remove yourself from this establishment with all haste!"

"Watch it, Sunbeam!" Ron growled, quite undeterred by Gerald's courtroom manner. "I'm just about mad enough to take it out on you as well as him!"

Gerald stood his ground and retorted, pompously.

"In that case, I should also warn you that if you attempt to lay a finger on that child or on me, we will not be discussing mere fines, but imprisonment!"

When even the threat of imprisonment failed to budge Ron Jenkins from his resolve to dispense his own brand of summary justice on the young offender, Gerald changed his tactics and tried reasoning with the man.

"Look, er . . ." he smiled, self-effacingly, ". . . let's discuss this man to man, shall we?" As his adversary scowled contemptuously at him, he continued. "I . . . . . . well, surely, it was a fair scrap between two healthy lads and . . ."

"Fair scrap!" Ron interjected, jabbing a grimy finger at Bill. "He fights dirty! Elbows, knees, putting the boot in, the lot!''

For a moment, Gerald stood rooted to the spot, shocked by the unsavoury stranger's allegations. Then he turned round to Bill and demanded:

"Is that true?"

Bill just shrugged his shoulders and grinned.

"I won, didn't I?"

Gerald pursed his lips and breathed in deeply before turning back to Ron.

"Very well!" he snapped, icily. "As soon as the boy's mother returns, I shall acquaint her with the facts and I can assure you that she will take appropriate disciplinary action."

Ron leered unpleasantly as he replied with heavy, laboured sarcasm in his voice.

"What will she do then? Send him to bed without any dinner? No pocket money for two weeks? Confiscate his train set?"

Stung by the stranger's nasty jibes, Gerald pulled himself to his full height and rounded frostily on him.

"There certainly won't be any question of corporal punishment, if that's what you mean!"

Ron threw up his hands impatiently and moved closer to Gerald.

"Look!" he reasoned. "You're not his father. It's nothing to you!"

He spat on his hands and rubbed them together in a gesture that signified that the time for talking had passed and the time for action had arrived. The four younger children watched, horror-stricken, as he bared his teeth into a menacing grin and began to advance on Bill. As Bill backed away from the murderous-looking creature moving towards him, Gerald stepped firmly in between them and stemmed the advance.

"His father is, unfortunately, dead," he said, putting out his hand to keep Ron at arm's length. "However, in this instance, I am standing in for same!"

Joanna, her courage returning now that the danger had momentarily passed, commented:

"And if my daddy was alive, he wouldn't let anyone frighten us all like he's doing!"

With one eye still on Ron, Gerald turned his head towards her and observed: "Joanna, your father would have said exactly what I am about to say." He turned to face Ron and once again tried to reason with him. "Now look! We both condemn the fact that the boys struck each other. However, as grown men, setting an example, I'm sure neither of us wish to escalate that violence."

Toby shook his head dolefully.

"He wouldn't have said that!" he said, looking to the others for confirmation of his statement.

"How do you know?" Gerald snapped shortly. "You're too young to know!"

"Well, I'm not," Richard chipped in. "My dad would have said to him, 'Get out or I'll throw you down the stairs!'"

Gerald's face took on an alarmed expression as he saw all the children nodding their heads vigorously in agreement. Ron was grinning maliciously at him.

"You want to try that, Sunbeam?" he said, prodding Gerald in the chest.

Gerald pushed his hand away, contemptuously.

"Certainly not! What would that prove?" he asked.

David shook his head, sadly.

"You're nothing like our dad," he sighed.

"Not one little bit," Joanna agreed.

Clearly irritated by the comparison, Gerald turned on them, sharply.

"I'm quite sure that your father would not have condoned what is tantamount to a back-street brawl," he snapped.

With his usual forthrightness, Toby voiced what was in all the children's minds at that moment.

"He wouldn't have been afraid of a fight!"

"Looking at that one," Ron interjected, indicating Toby with his thumb, "I can believe that!"

"You keep out of this!" Gerald hissed at Ron before turning back to Toby and reasoning, "Of course he

41

wouldn't have been afraid," He smiled almost apologetically at the children. "Neither, I can assure you, am I."
The expressions on the children's faces indicated that they were far from convinced by his assurance. His ego was a little deflated as he continued. "A fight? Well, let's analyse that, shall we? In the ring with the gloves on? The noble art of self-defence?" he laughed nervously. "Nothing wrong with that!"

The children were bored by what appeared to them just words from a chicken-livered, frightened man who wasn't a bit like the dad they remembered, and who'd do anything to avoid a fight. Their interest revived, however, when Ron responded.

"All right! If you want to settle it that way, it's okay with me!"

"Don't be ridiculous!" Gerald snorted.

Ron grinned at the children and then at Gerald.

"I thought you were standing up for these kids," he sneered.

"I most certainly am!" Gerald retorted indignantly.

As Gerald stood, breathing fire at his uncouth adversary, David stepped in and tried to be helpful.

"There's a gymnasium in the Youth Club just down the road!" he suggested.

"Yeah!" Richard added, eager to see them thumping hell out of each other. "They've got a boxing ring, gloves and everything!"

Ron's eyes gleamed maliciously as he latched onto the chance to satisfy his bloodlust.

"What time they open till?" he asked, licking his lips in anticipation of the slaughter he was about to perpetrate.

"Eight o'clock!" David enthused. "So there's plenty of time.

Gerald could hardly believe the evidence of his ears, and throughout the exchange between Ron and the boys, his head shot from side to side like a spectator at a tennis tournament. He turned to Ron, who was eyeing him up and down like a hangman measuring his victim for the drop.

42

"Are you seriously suggesting . . ."

"Look, Sunbeam!" Ron cut in. "You can't lose face by letting me give that little monster there the good hiding he deserves and I can't lose face by going back to my kid and telling him I didn't do nothing about him being beaten up because some toffee-nosed solicitor talked me out of it." He shrugged his shoulders. "All right! In the ring, Queensberry rules. That seems to be the solution, don't it?"

As Gerald stared back at him, he could feel the childrens' eyes boring into the back of his head. He was well and truly trapped.

"An hour from now suit you, Sunbeam?" Ron asked, grinning from ear to ear.

Gerald didn't reply immediately. He was thinking feverishly for a way to avoid the seemingly imminent bout of fisticuffs.

"I think it only fair to warn you," he said at last, "that I represented my University at Boxing."

The children groaned inwardly — he was just trying to chicken out and they were afraid they would be cheated out of their fun. Ron cottoned on to their feelings and turned to play to the gallery with an expression of mock seriousness on his face.

"My legs have just turned to jelly," he said, shaking his body into an exaggerated tremble. He waited a moment for the laughs, and when they didn't materialise, straightened himself back into his usual posture and glanced at his watch.

"Six o'clock then! Okay?" He glanced at Gerald and took his stony-faced silence as a mute acceptance of the inevitable. As he moved to the door, Adela, who had not understood a word of the heated exchange that had taken place, stepped forward, smilingly, to open the door.

"Thank you for coming!" she said, as he went out through the door.

Gerald stared after him in defeated silence, and as his footsteps died away down the stairs, turned to stare at the children, who in turn stared back at him. The long silence that ensued was eventually broken by Gerald.

"Very well," he said in a tone that implied that all was far from well. He moved to the door, opened it and turned in the doorway, determined to make a dramatic exit line. He stood for a moment in thought, but inspiration was totally lacking and the words just wouldn't come.

"Very well!" he repeated, going through the door and closing it behind him.

Bill waited for him to go out of earshot and then turned to organise the family in order to capitalize on the main bout of the evening.

"Right, David! Go down to the coffee bar and spread the word and tell 'em we want a good turn-out." He turned to Joanna, who was hovering excitedly at his elbow. "Joanna, you find Josh and give him all the 'gen'. He's sure to want to run a book on the fight; and you, Richard! Get down to the gym and make sure everything's ship-shape, the ring ropes tightened and see there's plenty of gloves available — in all sizes," he laughed maliciously. "We don't want Parish chickening out on a technicality! Toby, you can . . ."

The living room became a hubbub of frenzied excitement as Bill continued to give out his orders to his younger brothers and sister. If this didn't become a night to remember, it wouldn't be for the lack of trying.

Chapter Six

The Reluctant Hero

The last-minute promotional activity by the Lampert children had paid off, and Bill grinned with satisfaction as he peered through the outer darkness surrounding the ring. All the neighbouring children seemed to be there in the gymnasium, buzzing with excitement as they waited for the two combatants to step into the brightly lit area that would soon become the battleground.

Bill looked round at his three brothers, who were firmly established on the front row.

"Where's Joanna?" he asked.

"She's gone home," Toby replied. "She wouldn't stay after we'd sold the ice creams."

Bill shrugged his shoulders as he observed, reflectively:

"Yeah well, she's a girl, isn't she? Doesn't like the sight of blood!" He grinned in an expression of male chauvinism before going on to more practical matters. "How much did we make?" he asked.

"One pound and five pence," Toby replied.

"And what about the entrance fees, Richard?"

"Three pounds and seventy pence."

Bill held out his hand.

"Let's have it then! All of it!"

As they both handed him the money, Richard gave him a sly wink.

"Invest it wisely!" he said.

Bill didn't need telling what to do with the money. He knew how best to invest it and he was onto a certainty. He winked back at Richard and hurried away from the ringside.

David had rigged up an old record-player and the record

was already turning on the turntable. He sat with his hand poised, waiting for the signal from Bill to place the stylus on the record. Bill returned to the ring-side and, after glancing to the back of the crowd to ensure that the contestants were both in the hall, gave the signal for activities to commence. Right on cue, the Toreador song began to flood the hall.

Stand up and fight until you hear the bell,
Stand toe to toe,
Trade blow for blow,
Keep punching 'til you make those punches felt,
Show that crowd what you know —
Until you hear that bell
. . . that final bell —

Cheered by nearly forty lusty yelling voices, the two gladiators clambered up through the ropes into the ring. 'Battling' Ron Jenkins, smartly turned out in white singlet and shorts, looked every inch a bruiser and as he shadow-boxed in his corner, looked likely to live up to his billing. In complete contrast, Gerald, clad in a pair of old-fashioned rugger shorts and thin polo-necked sweater, cut a rather unprepossessing figure and unlikely to prove much of a match for the tough-looking character glowering at him from the opposite corner.

As Bill climbed up into the ring and put up his hands for silence, David took off the record and turned to Richard.

"I've got the *Last Post* ready!" he grinned.

"Keep it handy. You're going to need it," Richard replied.

Bill was grinning from ear to ear as he made the announcement.

"My Lords, Ladies and Gentlemen!" As the noise from the crowd died down, he pointed to Ron's corner. "In the red corner, 'Battling' Ron Jenkins . . ." He waited for the applause to die down and then indicated the opposite corner, ". . . and in the blue corner . . ."

The rest of the announcement was drowned by the premature clanging of the bell and he dodged out of the way as the two combatants came out of their respective corners. Late though the hour was, Gerald had still not given up hope of a relatively peaceful settlement and as they met in the centre of the ring, he said to Ron.

"First one to get knocked down is the loser, right?"

Ron leered at him from behind his gloves.

"Only if he hasn't got the guts to get up again."

Gerald held him at bay with his left hand as he reasoned.

"Look, we don't want to turn this into a bloodbath, do we?"

"I'm not worried," Ron taunted him. "It's going to be your blood!"

Gerald was getting exasperated, and made a last, desperate attempt to make the man see reason. To give greater emphasis to his words, he dropped his guard and extended both hands towards him as he appealed to his bloodthirsty adversary.

"What I'm trying to say is . . ."

That was as far as he got, for Ron, seeing his opponent with his guard down, saw this as an opportunity to put a summary end to the negotiations. Seizing his chance, he swung a vicious right hook which caught Gerald square on the side of the head and sent him toppling against the ropes. It was a sledgehammer blow, and had it not been for the ropes Gerald would certainly have hit the canvas. As he stood, shaking his head to clear his reeling senses, Ron, sensing the kill, turned and charged in at him like the wild bull of the pampas. The crowd roared as he aimed another murderous-looking hook at Gerald's jaw, and gasped with astonishment as Gerald ducked and the blow whistled harmlessly over his head. The impetus behind the punch almost threw Ron off balance, and before he could recover Gerald had slipped away from the ropes and danced quickly to the centre of the ring, where he took up a traditional stance.

Ron, having recovered his breath, glared at him menacingly.

"That was just for starters!" he snorted, as he began to advance towards him. He threw a couple of wild, haymaker punches, each of which Gerald avoided by swaying back out of reach and then, as Ron lumbered forward, neatly side-stepped, leaving Ron flailing the air with a whole battery of punches that all missed by a mile.

Gerald was still up on his toes, dancing in the centre of the ring, as Ron swung around, his face flushed with anger, and charged once more into the attack. He threw a lot of leather and became more and more furious as each punch failed to find its target.

As Gerald continued to bob and weave and duck and sway out of reach of Ron's fists, it became clear to the audience that he was playing with his opponent and giving him a much-needed boxing lesson, a fact that was not altogether appreciated by Ron, who was almost choking with rage as he continued to stomp around the ring, furiously lashing the air in all directions.

The crowd went wild with excitement as Gerald continued to give them a masterly display of defensive boxing and when, after one particularly violent attack from Ron, he side-stepped and tapped him playfully on the nose, they went almost hysterical with delight. It had the opposite effect on Ron and stung him into summoning all his remaining wind and strength into one last, vicious, haymaker of a punch, which, had it landed, would surely have knocked Gerald somewhere into the middle of the following week. Unfortunately for Ron, Gerald saw it coming a mile off and when he neatly side-stepped, Ron, unable to stop the momentum of the punch, spun round, lost his balance and ended up spreadeagled on the canvas.

As the crowd hooted with laughter, Gerald looked down and extended his hand to him.

"Had enough, old chap?" he asked.

Gerald's innocent question was like a red rag to a bull and galvanised Ron into near appoplexy. He scrambled to his feet and hurled himself at Gerald, desperately swinging punches with both hands. Gerald sighed, quickly sized him up and let fly with a perfect straight left that landed right on the button of Ron's chin. His legs wobbled and he went down like a sack of potatoes, out to the world.

No one bothered with the formality of a count. It wasn't necessary, for it was a full minute before the befuddled Ron began to stir on the canvas. Gerald stayed in the ring only long enough to see that his opponent was not seriously hurt, then he bounded out through the ropes, dressed, showered, and was out of the club within five minutes.

In the wild cheering crowd that applauded Gerald's victory, there were only four glum faces. The Lampert boys sat transfixed by the ringside, their faces paralysed with disappointment.

As Gerald left the club, he spotted the four of them sitting disconsolately on a low wall just outside. He still felt the flush of victory as he strode over to join them.

"Well, that showed him what's what, eh?"

His smile quickly evaporated as he beheld the gloomy faces of the four boys. "Why all the long faces?" he asked. "We won, didn't we?"

Bill scowled at him, accusingly.

"You won. We lost!"

Gerald was at a loss to understand the depressive attitude that confronted him. It just didn't make sense. He'd stepped in and saved Bill from Ron Jenkins and now he'd settled the score for him by knocking the man cold.

"Lost what?" he asked. "I fail to understand."

Toby shrugged his shoulders dejectedly.

"It doesn't matter."

"Of course it matters!" Gerald snorted. "Here am I, celebrating a quite brilliant victory, all by myself. That matters!" He looked from one to the other as he waited for an explanation. David hesitated for a moment, exchanged glances with his brothers, and then tried to explain.

"Well . . . the thing is, we thought you were going to lose."

Gerald looked at him blankly. That was no explanation for the pall of gloom that had descended on them. Their behaviour was quite illogical.

"Then you should be pleasantly surprised!"

They could see the irrefutable logic of Gerald's

reasoning, but were too concerned with their own predicament to give much thought to his feelings. Richard, however, did seek to justify the action they had taken.

"Well, you did try to crawl out of the fight."

Gerald cast his eyes upwards and threw up his hands in an impatient gesture.

"Only to save Ron what's his name the indignity of . . . well, you saw what just happened in the gym."

"Oh, come on!" Bill growled, sullenly. "You as good as told us you were going to lose the fight. Back in the house, you were shaking like a leaf."

"Shaking with anger!" Gerald corrected him, curtly. "You misread the symptoms."

David shrugged his shoulders.

"Didn't come over that way, so we blew the lot."

"Blew what lot?" Gerald frowned.

Richard didn't need to consult his notes to answer that one — they all knew precisely what they'd made out of the promotion, down to the last penny.

"The four pounds, seventy-five pence we made from the entrance money and ice creams, plus all the pocket money we had between us. Ten pounds, seventeen pence in all," he lamented. "We bet you to lose."

Gerald froze indignantly.

"Really!" he snapped. "Well, it serves you damned well right!"

His sense of moral outrage was completely lost on young Toby, who stuck his chin out belligerently as he challenged him.

"Now what are we going to do for the rest of the holidays without any money?"

Gerald glared at him frostily.

"That is hardly my concern!" he snorted. He stood for a moment, breathing thunder, then gave them a last withering look before turning on his heel and stalking away from them in high dudgeon.

He was still feeling rattled when he got back to the house, and went straight down the hall to his deserted office, strode through to his own room and stood, glaring up at the portrait of his father on the wall.

"A wonderful time we've been having, me and my ever loving family." He smiled without humour as he continued to vent his spleen at the portrait. "Fun and Games down in the gym provided the final, sensational, once in a lifetime climax to the day. 'What did it achieve?' I hear you ask." He smiled bitterly. "Well I'll tell you. Nothing!" He began to pace the room, glancing across at the portrait as he continued to address it. "You see, dear father, I have a problem. A tiny, miniscule problem that's hardly worth mentioning." He made an elaborate gesture of introduction to the portrait as he mimed the fearful possibility that was uppermost in his mind. "Oh, father — this is Bill, my eldest son, as you know from my letters. Charming lad. His idea of solving problems of personal relationships is a quick punch in the face, a kick on the shin, and if all else fails, a knee in the groin. Knowing your views on the question of law and order, I feel sure you're going to take your first grandchild to your heart and heartily approve of the way I've brought him up."

He was suddenly aware of the telephone ringing in his office.

"Ungrateful little . . ." he boiled with anger as he strode back into his office. "They're a lot of ill-mannered hooligans!" He snatched the receiver off its hook.

"Yes!" he snapped.

"Gerald?" his father's voice barked at the other end of the line.

He swallowed hard as he tried to force sweet reason back into his voice.

"Yes, hello sir!"

Without wasting words on pleasantries, Parish senior went straight on to inform him of yet another change of plan.

"Flight number and arrival time the same, but I'll be over earlier," he announced. "Next Saturday, in fact. Got it?"

"Next Saturday?" Gerald gulped blankly. "That's four days from now!"

"I'm aware of that, you idiot!" the old man blasted in his ear. "I can count! Just fix up the car to meet me at the airport and tell your family to stand by. As far as you're concerned," he went on, "I still think the idea of your being away on holiday is a good one."

Before Gerald could reply, the phone slammed down at the other end. An agonised look came over his face as he slowly put down the receiver on its rest.

In the Lamperts' livingroom, Bill was engaged in a game of draughts with Richard, while the other children busied themselves pursuing their own various activities.

There was an unexpected tap on the door, but before anyone had time to answer it, the door opened and Gerald stepped into the room.

"Sorry to intrude . . ." he smiled.

The children all stopped what they were doing and stared, utterly bewildered by his constant change of attitude. He crossed over to them, quite undeterred by the strange looks they gave him.

"I've been thinking . . ." he began, taking his wallet from his pocket. "It is possible I could have given you the wrong impression about the outcome of the fight . . . not intentionally, I can assure you, but . . ." He opened the wallet and started to count out some notes into his hand. "How much did you say you lost? Ten pounds, wasn't it?"

"And seventeen pence!" Richard added quickly.

Gerald shrugged his shoulders as he smilingly handed a wad of pound notes to Bill.

"Call it eleven pounds, shall we?"

Chapter Seven

The Reject

For Mary Lampert, life sometimes seemed just one mad, continuous scramble of work, sleep and more work. Being the only breadwinner in the family left her little time to relax with her children, and the limited time she could spend with them always seemed taken up with her nagging and chivvying them to clear up the messes they created and bullying them to help Adela with the house-work. It was breakfast-time again and like every other working day, she had been racing against the clock to get everything organised at home before dashing off to the office to start her day's work.

As she crossed to the door, she saw Toby with his feet up on the sofa. "Toby, take your feet off the sofa!" she snapped. She opened the door and turned, taut-faced, to the children.

"Bye . . . See you all later!"

In the chorus of 'goodbyes' from the children, Toby's voice was a little subdued. His mother had been rather short-tempered with him and he took it very much to heart. He was the baby of the family. There was at least a four-year age-gap between him and the others. His brothers and sister were all much closer together. He was always the 'kid brother' and far too young to take part in their more grown-up games, but still old enough to run errands and do their bidding and take all the kicks they administered from time to time. Sometimes he felt very lonely, and never more so than on those occasions when his mother seemed to be angry with him. He watched sullenly as she went out of the room and as the door closed behind her, curled up on the sofa and began to thumb listlessly through the pages of a book. Joanna spotted him as she came down the stairs.

"That's my book on house-plants!" she snapped, snatching the book from him.

"Can't I just look through it?" he pleaded.

"No," she said, cattily. "You'll only lose it, or spill orange squash over it, or something."

Toby wrinkled his nose as he watched his sister flounce away with the book in her hand, got up from the sofa and crossed over to the table, where Richard was struggling to complete a half-finished jigsaw puzzle.

"Can I do it with you?" he asked.

Richard had a piece of the puzzle in his hand and was deep in concentration as he tried to find the correct place for it.

"No . . . Go away," he snapped, irritably.

Toby's face fell, but as he turned away from Richard, he saw fresh hope in David coming down the stairs, carrying a most complicated-looking model crane in his hands. It looked a beautiful model and was obviously nearing completion. His eyes lit up as he crossed over to meet his brother at the foot of the stairs.

"Can I help you with that?" he asked eagerly.

"No." David brushed past him and placed the model carefully down on the dining table, opposite Richard. Toby followed after him.

"Why not?"

"Because I'm entering it for a competition and it has to be delivered by tomorrow and if you helped I'd be lucky to get it finished this year," David replied as he turned away from Toby and started to work on the model.

Toby scowled and wandered aimlessly over to Bill, who was writing in an exercise book.

"What are you writing?"

Bill didn't look up as he replied:

"An essay."

"What about?" Toby asked.

Bill's concentration was broken by Toby's pestering and he was clearly irritated.

"About what to do to little seven-year-old brothers who are pests!" he snorted. "Like boiling them in oil! Go away!"

They were all being beastly to him and he felt thoroughly unwanted. It wasn't his fault he was so much younger than they were and anyhow, he could do most things as well as they could. Just because he was younger, did they think he had no feelings? He stood kicking his heels for a moment, but then his attention was attracted by a faint whirring sound coming from the table where David was working on his model crane. He watched, fascinated, as it swivelled, lowered its grapple, picked up a 'Dinky' car and deposited it neatly on top of a model 'transporter'. He crossed excitedly over to the table and stood behind David, who was operating the crane by means of a remote control he held in his hand.

Toby was itching to get his hands on the crane.

"Can I have a go?" he asked eagerly.

David turned on him sharply.

"Don't touch it!" he shouted.

Shocked by David's violent reaction, Toby started back as if he'd been shot. David relaxed as his 'kid brother' stood away from his creation, and announced proudly: "That is going to win me a trip to America. To Cape Canaveral. A week going over the whole Interspace System, including a trial in the Moon Rocket Simulator."

Toby was still smarting from his brother's reaction and didn't feel very charitable towards him.

"Bully for you!" he choked, turning away and crossing to the stairs. He looked back over his shoulder and could see his brothers and sister fully engrossed in what they were doing — they didn't even notice him. Feeling utterly rejected and unwanted, he crept slowly up the stairs to his room.

It was a couple of hours before he came down again and Adela was clearing away the coffee cups.

"What about me?" he asked, looking around at the others.

"Too late, as usual," Bill replied. "Elevenses are at

eleven o'clock.''

"But nobody called me!" he protested.

David crossed over to join in the baiting.

"You've got a watch," he said, winking at Bill, who was grinning all over his face.

"It's broken," Toby said, then clutching hopefully at straws, asked David, "Can you mend it?"

"Sorry," David laughed as he turned away and joined Bill on the sofa.

Toby blinked back tears; then, after a few moments, his expression hardened and his mouth set into a determined line.

"Right!" he muttered through his teeth, backing out of the room and scurrying up the stairs to his bedroom. He spent a frenzied few minutes throwing things from his wardrobe into a large plastic bag and crept down the stairs, struggling with the enormous burden on his shoulder. The others glanced across at him as he dropped his load at the bottom of the stairs and took a breather.

"Been having a clear-out," he lied glibly. "Just going to empty all this rubbish in the dustbin."

They weren't really interested in his explanation and whatever he was doing was all right by them as long as it kept their pest of a kid brother out of their hair. As they nodded and went back to their various activities, he struggled over to the door and dragged the plastic bag out onto the landing, closing the door behind him. Once on the landing, he opened the bag and took from it a small suitcase and some items of outdoor clothing. He quickly donned coat, hat and gloves, stuffed the plastic bag behind one of Joanna's plants, picked up the suitcase and started to descend the stairs.

He was negotiating the last flight when the front door opened and Gerald came into the house. The sight of Toby in outdoor clothes, suitcase in hand, threading his way down through the greenery and the sombre expression on his face caused Gerald to stop and stare.

"You er . . . going somewhere?" he asked.

Toby took the last few steps to the hall and walked

straight past Gerald to the front door.

"I'm leaving home," he mumbled, as he struggled to open the door.

Gerald smiled to himself and decided to humour him.

"Oh I see," he said, assuming an expression of mock gravity. "Do you have any idea where you'll be staying?"

Toby turned in the doorway and gave serious consideration to Gerald's question before replying thoughtfully, "I haven't quite decided yet," adding after a moment's pause, "Somewhere in London." He picked up his suitcase and went through the door. "Goodbye Mr Parish!" he called as he closed the door behind him.

"Going to London. Huh!" Gerald chuckled to himself as he went down the hall to his office. He was so tickled by the ridiculousness of the idea that he was still laughing as he went through the outer office to his own room.

"Come on through, will you Nesta!" he laughed over his shoulder as he proceeded to sit down at his desk. His alarmed-looking secretary hurriedly exchanged her knitting for a note-pad and scurried into the room and sat down opposite to him. He quickly pulled himself together and assumed a business-like attitude.

"Letter to Messrs. Bugle, Losey and Cranroach," he began, and went on to dictate. "Dear Sirs, reference fifty-one Shackleton Avenue . . ." He broke off momentarily as Nesta scribbled away to catch up with him.

"He wouldn't really be running away, would he?" His brow puckered as he considered the reply to his own question and then he shook his head and reassured himself. "No!" Then he turned back to Nesta and continued to dictate. "With regard to your claim that my client has erected a chain-link fence encroaching on your client's land . . ." Nesta was scribbling furiously, and he paused to let her catch up again.

"It would be a bit embarrassing if he really had gone off to London," he mused to himself as the alarming consequences of such a happening began to flash through his mind. Though not altogether indifferent to the fate of the young seven-year-old bane of his existence, his

57

main fears centred on the reaction of Parish senior on finding one of his brood of 'grandchildren' missing from the hatch. He shook his head again and sought to find reassurance in the impossibility of such a thing happening. "What am I thinking about? The whole thing's ridiculous!" He took a deep breath and turned back to Nesta, who had caught up with his dictation and was sitting with pencil poised, waiting for him to continue.

"I have personally inspected the alleged encroachment and, having measured the distance to the inch, I can assure you that . . ." Nesta was again scratching away frantically to keep up with him, and as he paused to allow her to catch up, his eyes wandered over to the picture on the wall. "I must be mad!" he fretted. "I can't take that chance with you coming over next week." His thoughts flashed to the letters he had written to his father. "Five children, I said, not four! Oh to hell with it." He put his hand to his head and tried to dispel such depressive thoughts from his mind. As he glanced at Nesta across the desk, she was looking at him with a wild, triumphant expression on her face that told him she had caught up and was waiting for him to go on with the letter.

"No court of law in the country . . ." he went on, ". . . would uphold the absurd accusations your client is levelling at . . ." his eyes wandered back to the portrait and he suddenly exclaimed, "My God, I can't really take that chance, can I?"

He suddenly got up from his chair and put his hand to his head:

"I won't be a moment, Nesta, I'm just . . ." His knees began to wobble and he put his hands forward onto the desk to steady himself, before collapsing back into his chair. Nesta watched anxiously as he took a handkerchief from his pocket and mopped his brow. There was a strange, haunted look in his eyes as he automatically folded the handkerchief and put it back into his pocket. He smiled, painfully, across the desk at her.

"We might as well finish this letter off first," he sighed. "Now, where was I?"

Her thin lips winced into a smile as she cleared her throat and prepared to read from her pad.

"Dear Sirs," she began, coughing again to remove the persistent frog from her throat. ". . . Reference fifty-one Shackleton Avenue. He really wouldn't be running away, would he? No! With regard to your claim that my client has erected a chain link fence encroaching on your client's land, it would be a bit embarrassing if he really has gone off to London. What am I talking about? The whole thing's ridiculous!" She paused for breath, glanced across the desk, and quite undeterred by the blank look of utter, dumbstruck amazement on Gerald's face, continued to read from her notes. "I have personally inspected the alleged encroachment and having measured the distance to the inch, I can assure you that I must be mad. I can't afford to take the chance with you coming over next week. Five children, I said, not four. Oh to hell with it! No Court of Law in the country would uphold the absurd accusations your client is levelling at my God. I really can't take the chance, can I?"

Gerald was still staring at her in total disbelief as she looked up from her notebook, waiting for him to continue dictating the letter. It was some moments before his power of speech returned. He rose to his feet, swallowed hard and addressed her in tones of controlled fury.

"Nesta, I can't remember exactly how much it is I pay you every week, but whatever it is, it's too much!" He quivered self-righteously to his full height, took a deep breath and strode out through the outer office into the hall, leaving a very confused Nesta staring after him.

Upstairs, in the Lamberts' living-room, the children were quietly engrossed in a game of monopoly. There was a tap on the front door and as they all looked round a breathless Gerald burst into the room.

"I er . . . I know this sounds absurd," he stammered, "but I met Toby in the hall a few minutes ago and er . . well, he had a suitcase, and said he was leaving home . . . running away. Preposterous of course."

David cast his eyes upwards as he groaned.

"Oh no! Not again!"

Gerald turned round quickly to face him.

"Again?" he echoed.

Bill was sprawling back on the sofa.

"He's always running away," he said, nonchalantly.

Disturbed by their apparent lack of concern for their seven-year-old brother, Gerald gestured impatiently.

"Well, he can't have got very far. If we . . ."

He was interrupted by Richard, who laughingly exclaimed.

"You don't know Toby. He flags down the first car that passes."

David nodded his head in agreement, adding:

"The forlorn little boy with the angelic smile . . ."

"And the persuasive tongue," Joanna chipped in. "He's had them driving him all over the place."

"And us running around in circles all day." Bill yawned as he resignedly staggered to his feet. "Okay, Richard, you check out the coffee bar just in case; David, the bus depot, and you, Joanna, all his friends who live locally. I'll cover the railway station." He crossed over to the telephone. "First of all, I'd better alert the airport!"

"The airport!" Gerald gasped.

Bill didn't need to look up the number, and dialled it automatically as he talked to Gerald.

"We once caught up with him three minutes before he boarded a scheduled flight to Athens."

"But how did he get a ticket?" Gerald stammered as the others hurried out of the room. He could hear the number ringing out from the receiver in Bill's hand.

"Spun them some tale about having lost it . . ." As a voice answered at the other end of the line, Bill broke off and put the receiver to his ear. "Hello, Mr Rogers?" He glanced over at Gerald and sighed. "Oh hello, Mr Rogers . . . Yes, it's Toby again!"

Gerald's brow was furrowed as he pondered on the problem of the missing boy, then, suddenly, an obvious thought flashed across his mind and galvanised him into action.

"The police!" he exclaimed. "That's who we need. I'll call the police!" He dashed out of the room, leaving Bill still wearily relating the details of Toby's latest disappearance to the airport authorities.

Chapter Eight

The New Lodger

Gerald plunged down through the greenery to the ground floor with such reckless abandon that some of it was still hanging round his neck as he rushed through the outer office to his room. A very startled Nesta exclaimed:

"Mr Parish . . . !"

He had already flashed past her and had snatched the phone on his desk from its rest without registering the small boy sitting demurely in a chair at the side of Nesta's desk. He started to dial the number.

"Nine — nine — ni. . ." He suddenly stopped as the vision of Toby, sitting down in the adjoining room, caught up with him. Or was it imagination? He put the telephone down slowly onto its rest and turned and stared through the open door into the outer office.

"Toby!" he gasped, unbelievingly.

It was no figment of Gerald's imagination that got up and walked into his office.

"I . . . I thought you were running away," Gerald stammered, as Toby closed the door behind him. "London, I think you said."

"I am!" Toby replied, crossing over and sitting down near the desk. "But first, I wanted to discuss some business with you."

"Business?" Gerald blinked at the self-possessed little fellow sitting opposite to him. "Oh, very well," he said, leaning forward in his seat to listen to his young client's proposition.

Toby wasted no time on small talk.

"I've got two pounds, sixteen pence . . ." he began, pitching straight into the crux of the problem, ". . . and that's not enough for the train fare, so I'd like to borrow ten pounds, which will make twelve pounds, sixteen pence, which will cover my fare and leave enough over to live on until I find a job.''

Gerald smiled at the thought of the diminutive seven-year-old looking for a job in London. The idea was utterly ridiculous, but as he looked across the desk, there could be no doubt that young Toby was in deadly earnest. He tried to humour him.

''But you can't just . . .'' That was as far as he got before Toby took off his wrist-watch and reached across the desk to slap it down in front of him.

''The loan will be against the security of my watch.''

''But you can't just . . . go to London,'' Gerald tried to reason. ''What about your mother?''

''I'll write to her every day,'' came the innocent reply. Gerald was getting rapidly out of his depth.

''But — but what on earth do you imagine you're going to do in London?'' he spluttered. ''What sort of job do you think you're going to get?''

''I'm going to be a chef,'' Toby replied without hesitation.

''Aren't you a little young for that?'' Gerald quizzed. Toby looked at him, scornfully.

''You don't become a chef overnight. You have to train to be one.''

The boy was trying to teach his grandmother to suck eggs, for there was little Gerald didn't know about the world of haute cuisine. He bristled slightly and assumed the air of the man who knows.

''You also have to be considerably older,'' he corrected the would-be novice, posing the question with a superior smile. ''You intend training for the next ten years?''

The wind visibly went out of Toby's sails.

''Who told you it would take ten years?'' he asked anxiously.

Gerald laughed disarmingly.

''Oh, you don't have to take my word for it, Toby!'' He waved his arm over in the direction of the telephone.

"Ring any of the big restaurants! Go on, there's the phone! Ring the Savoy and ask them!"

Toby stared at him in silence, utterly deflated by Gerald's confident tone.

"Go on, ring them!" Gerald urged him.

Toby rose slowly to his feet and moved round the desk to the telephone. He put his hand on the receiver, then suddenly withdrew it and swung round to face Gerald.

"I'm not going back upstairs!" he cried excitedly. "I hate them! I hate them all!"

The boy was near to tears, and in spite of himself Gerald felt the stirring of compassion in his breast.

"Oh, come now, Toby!" he said, soothingly, but the boy was not to be so easily deflected from his resolve to leave home.

"I'm not going back to live with those rotten brothers of mine who won't let me play with them and that rotten sister who won't even let me look at her book!" he sobbed.

Gerald got up, put his hand on Toby's shoulder and tried to pour oil on troubled waters.

"I'm sure you're over-reacting to what is really a slight misunderstanding which often . . ."

Toby cut in on him tearfully.

"If I can't go to London and become a chef, I'm darned well going somewhere and you can't stop me." He broke away and headed for the door but was prevented from going out by Gerald, who nipped round smartly and barred his way.

"You can't keep me here forever," Toby shouted defiantly, and as Gerald tried to reason with him, threatened, "I'll kick your ankles."

There was no doubt in Gerald's mind that the young man meant business and since he had no desire to be hacked on the ankles, stretched out his arm to keep his would-be assailant at bay and his legs out of kicking distance of Toby's small but sturdily shod feet.

It was a desperate situation that called for a desperate remedy, though not perhaps quite as desperate as the remedy which flashed into Gerald's mind at that moment.

"Look!" he cried desperately, struggling to keep Toby at arm's length. "If you absolutely insist on not going back to your family, you can . . ." The struggling stopped suddenly as Gerald took a deep breath and forced out the rest of the sentence. "You can stay with me."

"With you?" Toby stared unbelievingly for a few moments before the sceptical side of his nature took over and produced a rational reaction. He shrugged and nodded up at the ceiling. "But you're worse than they are!" he said.

Gerald's conversion over the previous few days may have been dictated by purely selfish considerations, but notwithstanding, Toby's rejection of his offer of hospitality cut him to the quick.

"Thank you very much!" he fumed indignantly. "I offer you a sanctuary. I agree to allow you to stay in my home and you . . ." His speech was becoming incoherent and he was forced to pause to allow his boiling sense of moral outrage to simmer down. As he regained control over his vocal chords, he asked in a tone of injured self-righteousness, "What kind of gratitude is that?"

There was no response from Toby, who shuffled his feet uncomfortably as he gazed sheepishly at the floor. Gerald held the pose for some considerable time, but then, when no apology was forthcoming, snapped irritably:

"All right! Go on! Go to London! Go where you like!" He took his wallet from his pocket and extracted a ten pound note. "Here!" he said, offering the money to Toby. "You need the money for the rail fare . . . Ten pounds! Don't think of it as a loan. It's a gift! Now get out of here!"

Toby's eyes flickered up at him for a moment, then he shook his head and continued to stare at the ground.

"Well?" Gerald demanded.

There was a moment's pause before Toby looked up shamefacedly and mumbled, quietly:

"Perhaps I shouldn't have said you were worse than that lot upstairs."

Gerald inflated visibly as he pompously prepared himself to accept an apology, nodding his head indulgently as Toby went on to qualify his withdrawal.

"You have been behaving a little better lately."

The hidden barb in Toby's observation brought a delayed reaction from Gerald, causing him to stiffen and frown slightly, as he pondered on the backhanded compliment. He glanced uncertainly at Toby, whose face was suddenly wreathed in smiles.

"Okay. I'll stay with you," the youngster conceded generously, picking up his suitcase and moving to the door. "See you later Mr Parish!" he called cheerfully, as he went out of the room.

As the door closed behind him, Gerald mopped his brow and gazed up at the framed portrait of his father.

"My God!" he exclaimed with feeling. "What are you doing to me?"

Mary had only been back in the flat for a few minutes and was distraught with worry over the disappearance of Toby. She prowled up and down the room, berating the other crestfallen children, who had been searching for their young brother non-stop from the moment they had missed him, without any success.

". . . I suppose you've all been having a go at him again," she ranted. "Can't you get it into your heads that he's still only a baby!"

"A baby!" Bill snorted scornfully, but before he could elaborate Mary swung round on him furiously.

"He's the baby of this family and you lot kick him about . . ."

"We never touched him!" Richard protested. "He was just wandering around being his normal self."

"And what does that mean?" Mary snapped, belligerently.

"A damned nuisance!" Bill muttered.

"And he took my book!" Joanna whined.

Mary put her hand to her head and exploded.

"For heaven's sake, Joanna! What about all the times you've taken things of mine? I spend half my life looking for needles and cottons and knitting wool and a hundred

66

other things and where do I inevitably find them?'' Joanna turned away as her mother hammered home the point. ''In your room!'' Without pausing for breath, she turned to glare at all of them. ''You've all behaved abominably!'' she admonished them.

The rocket had gone home and they shuffled uneasily, avoiding her gaze as she looked from one to the other.

''Right!'' she demanded. ''Now, where is he?''

The ensuing silence was broken when a discreet cough brought them all round to face Gerald, who was standing in the open doorway.

''Excuse me!'' he smiled, ''but I think I may be able to be of some assistance.'' He advanced reassuringly into the room. ''Well, actually, Toby is downstairs in my flat.''

Mary rushed forward, tears of relief and joy welling up in her eyes.

''Oh thank you Mr Parish!'' she was already over by the door. ''I'll make quite sure that he doesn't bother you a moment longer.'' She hurried out of the room and was soon picking her way down the stairs through the plants, with Gerald in hot pursuit.

''Well, the situation is slightly complicated by the fact that . . .'' Gerald panted as he tried to catch up with her. ''Er . . . I was just wondering . . .''

She glanced back reassuringly over her shoulder.

''Don't worry!'' she cut in. ''I'll have him out of there in two shakes of a lamb's tail.''

''It's partly my fault,'' Gerald added quickly, side-stepping a large plant-pot on the bottom flight. ''Perhaps I shouldn't have done, but I did promise Toby . . .'' As Mary reached the bottom stair, Gerald was several steps behind her and had to rush to catch up with her. ''The thing is I . . .'' he gasped, putting out his hand to restrain her. ''. . . that is, he, Toby . . . er . . . What I'm trying to say is that I sort of promised that he could stay with me.''

Mary stopped in her tracks and turned to face him, a look of blank amazement on her face.

''But you don't want to have Toby . . .'' She broke

off as Gerald raised his hand against her objection and cut across her.

"By this time tomorrow," he smiled reassuringly, "he'll be so bored that he'll be begging to go back upstairs." He beamed as Mary hesitated in the hall, assuring her confidently, "You'll see. He'll be back with you tomorrow, and glad to be." He chuckled as he went on to visualise the scene inside his flat. "Even at this moment, he's probably wandering aimlessly around my flat, regretting the whole thing," he mused, taking her arm and leading her back to the foot of the stairs.

Mary smiled up at him, hesitated for a moment, then turned and began to move slowly up the stairs, through the greenery to the flat above. Gerald watched after her until she went out of his sight on the top landing, sighed, and, shaking his head reflectively, turned and wandered across the hall to the door of his own flat.

Chapter Nine

The Banquet

Gerald was still deep in thought as he went in through the door into his flat, yet there was nothing depressive about the thoughts that were going through his mind. On the contrary, he felt strangely elated and was humming to himself as he stepped carefully over the toys that littered his otherwise impeccably tidy room. Mary was certainly an attractive woman and it was strange that he'd never noticed it before, but then again why should he have noticed? He was a confirmed bachelor and the very idea of forming any sort of permanent liaison with a woman had never featured in his plans. The idea was really quite unthinkable — a widow with a brood of five children. He pushed the thought to the back of his mind and began to contemplate one of the more tangible delights of bachelordom — gourmandising alone with exotic dishes, prepared and cooked to perfection as only he knew how. Tonight, however, he wouldn't be alone. He'd have to share his culinary creations with Toby. It was regrettable, but it would only be for one night and he would at least be able to introduce the boy to haute cuisine as it should be.

He looked around, but there was no sign of Toby.

"Toby?" he called out.

"In the kitchen," Toby's voice answered.

Gerald sighed with relief that the wanderer had not disappeared again and made towards the kitchen.

"I have a surprise for you!" he announced. "Filet de Boeuf de Maître d'Hotel. A gastronomic delight. I shall cook you a meal tonight that you will remember for the rest of your li. . ." He broke off suddenly as he reached the open kitchen door and froze with horror at the scene he beheld. The place was an absolute tip, hardly recognisable as the immaculately kept kitchen Gerald had left an hour or so earlier. In the midst of all the flour, butter and utensils that littered every working surface, Toby, dressed up in Gerald's striped apron, was clearly having the time of his life. He was busily putting meat through the mincer, and at his side, lying sadly in the mixing bowl, was a great unsavoury-looking lump of yellow dough.

"What on earth are you doing?" Gerald gasped in horror.

Toby grinned from ear to ear as he proudly showed him the bowl of minced steak.

"Minced steak!" he announced. "For minced-meat pie!"

The self-control Gerald had acquired during the past few days suddenly evaporated as he beheld what had happened to his cherished Filet de Boeuf. His face went a deep shade of purple as he exploded:

"You've just destroyed a pound and a half of Scotch beef hung to perfection!"

"It was the only meat I could find," Toby shrugged.

Gerald pulled himself together and determined to make the best of the situation. He crossed over and examined the minced steak more closely.

"Alright!" he said, as philosophically as his shattered nerves would allow. "We'll have to make do with Steak Tartare."

That was a completely new one to Toby and his young brow furrowed as he asked:

"How do you cook that?"

"You don't," Gerald replied. "You eat it raw."

Toby was horror-stricken.

"I'm not going to eat raw meat!" he exclaimed. "That gives you worms. Besides," he said, pointing over to the big mixing bowl, "look at the lovely pastry I've made!"

Gerald sickened as he gazed at the menacing-looking yellow cannon ball lying in the bowl.

"Good God!" he gasped.

Since Toby had made the pastry with his own fair hands,

he didn't quite grasp the significance of Gerald's remark and shrugged it off, inviting Gerald to leave him alone to get on with his creation.

"You go and sit down," he urged, adding, "Mum always says two can't share a kitchen."

The tensions that had been building up in Gerald suddenly exploded into a near-violent, uncontrolled outburst.

"I'm not sharing my kitchen with you! I'm not sharing my kitchen with anyone!" he yelled. "Get out! Get out of my kitchen! Get out of my flat!"

Toby watched, unbelievingly, as Gerald gestured wildly in the direction of the door. It was all so unfair and he was hurt and bewildered by Gerald's lack of appreciation of his efforts.

"All right, I will," he pouted, slowly untying his apron strings. "I'll do what I was going to do in the first place. I'll go to London!"

The thought of the boy disappearing again clarified Gerald's confused mind with remarkable rapidity.

"No," he cried, fighting with all his will-power to retain his calm. "You see . . . I've had rather a trying day!" he said, rushing over and retying Toby's apron strings. "Yes . . . pressure of work," he smiled wearily. "You understand?" He backed away to the kitchen door. "You just carry on," he said, forcing a smile to his lips. "Minced-meat pie sounds just fine . . . just the thing." He closed the kitchen door behind him, put his hand to his brow and stood for a few moments with his back against the door. Then he stood up straight and strode over to the drinks tray, stumbling and nearly breaking his neck on one of Toby's scattered toys on the way. He took a large tumbler, poured himself a very large Scotch and downed half of it in one gulp. He turned suddenly and shouted towards the kitchen.

"I'll just tidy up in here, shall I?"

Toby's shrill voice came piercing back through the closed door.

"When you've done that, can you lay the table?"

He closed his eyes in despair, picked up the glass and downed the remaining half of his drink.

Gerald's senses were numbed by the Scotch as he cleared up the toys left on the floor by Toby, but not sufficiently numbed to dispel his dread of the impending meal. He laid the table and sat down, racking his brains for a plausible excuse to avoid the necessity of actually having to eat the unappetizing mess Toby was cooking. All too soon, Toby's head appeared round the kitchen doorway.

"Dinner's ready!" he announced as he came into the room.

Gerald jumped to his feet and glanced anxiously at his watch.

"It's only just gone six!" he exclaimed, adding hastily, "I never eat before eight!"

"Well I do and I'm starving," Toby replied. He looked approvingly at the seating arrangement at the dining table and then frowned. "Where's the bottle of tomato sauce?" he asked reprovingly.

Gerald was clearly scandalised.

"Bottle?" he snorted, scathingly. "Sauces are made, not bottled!"

Toby breathed in deeply, cast his eyes to the ceiling and nodding patiently.

"Of course I know they have to be made before they're put into bottles."

Gerald couldn't deny the irrefutable logic in Toby's remark but, as a gourmet, couldn't allow such an obvious heresy to go unchallenged.

"My dear Toby!" His speech was slightly slurred but this impediment did nothing to lessen the faint note of condescension in his voice. "Food," he pronounced solemnly, "is a mundane necessity of life, but to turn manna into ambrosia ... the sauce!" He paused dramatically before going on to elaborate on the alchemistic properties of the sauce. "The sauce to tantalise and titivate the tastebuds with delicate undertones of deliciousness, adding sophisticated relish, indefinable

72

suggestions of piquancy to the simple ingredients of sustenance. That is art! And it does not come out of a bottle!"

There was an expression of utter boredom on Toby's face as he waited for Gerald to finish his peroration. Then he shrugged his shoulders and sighed wearily.

"You haven't got any tomato sauce."

"No I have not!" Gerald snorted indignantly.

"Ah well," Toby replied, making the best of a bad job. "I'll go out and buy some tomorrow."

Gerald watched him disappear back into the kitchen before plunging over to the drinks tray and pouring himself another stiff Scotch. Before he could get the glass to his lips, Toby had returned with a saucepan in one hand and an enormous serving spoon in the other.

"You do like potatoes, don't you?" he asked, and before Gerald could answer, had doled out a vast quantity of lumpy, semi-mashed potato onto his plate. He then served himself a similar amount and went back with the empty saucepan to the kitchen. Gerald stared in morbid fascination at the slag-heap of potatoes on his plate, gave them an exploratory prod with his fork and recoiled with horror as Toby returned with another saucepan in his hand.

"Greens! Good for you!" he grinned, plonking a huge spoonful of the scraggy-looking cabbage onto Gerald's plate, and going on to serve himself with an equally generous portion before returning to the kitchen for his pièce de résistance.

Gerald gulped and swallowed hard as he watched Toby bring in the evil-smelling mince-meat pie. The thought of having to eat it brought him out in a cold, nervous sweat.

"Just look at that!" Toby said, proudly, as he placed it carefully down on the serving mat and stood back to reveal his masterpiece.

Gerald needed no bidding to look at it, for as he stood, clutching his glass, his eyes were glued to the charred, grey, soggy-looking mess on the table. The nauseating smell of stewed cabbage mingling with the unpleasant aroma of burnt, half-baked pastry was having a claustrophobic effect on him, and he would have obeyed his instinct to run, screaming, out into the fresh air, had it not been for a strange paralysis that was seeping into and seizing his joints. His head was swimming, and there was a hard lump in his throat which all his hard swallowing had failed to dislodge and which, alarmingly, seemed to be getting larger with every second.

Quite unaware of the agonies Gerald was suffering, Toby sat down at the table and, licking his lips in anticipation of the banquet before him, plunged his knife into the sad, grey centre of the pie, hacked his way through the burnt, unyielding edges, and with the help of a huge serving spoon conveyed an enormous portion to his plate. He looked up at Gerald, who was still teetering on the brink.

"You're not going to eat standing up, are you?" he asked, taking a huge mouthful of the pie from his fork.

Gerald averted his gaze from the pie, closed his eyes and in a sudden movement downed his Scotch in one.

"It's very kind of you to have gone to all this trouble, Toby," he stammered, light-headedly, "but the fact is I'm not feeling awfully well."

Toby stopped eating for a moment and stared up at him.

"I'm not surprised," he said chidingly. "Do you always drink like that?"

Gerald glanced down at the glass in his hand.

"Oh no! I just felt a strong desire to . . ." He broke off suddenly and decided to take the bull by the horns. "Look, if you don't mind, I'll just nibble at a Bath Oliver and a piece of Camembert."

Toby shook his head, sadly.

"Ah well, you can have cold pie and bubble and squeak tomorrow," he sighed, before shrugging his shoulders and returning with renewed gusto to the task in hand.

Having won a short reprieve, Gerald sat down at the table and as he nibbled at his Bath Oliver, was filled with uneasy wonder as he watched the plateful of garbage disappear into Toby's stomach. Uncharitably, and with little thought for Toby's overloaded digestive organs, he glanced at the remainder of the pie and hoped the boy's appetite would prove insatiable.

Chapter Ten

The Prodigal's Return

After several days without a square meal inside him, Gerald was not at all convinced as to the therapeutic effects of fasting. His hunger grew day by day and it was a matter of growing concern to him, how long he could go on resisting the nightly meals of unwholesome garbage prepared by Toby in his kitchen.

For his part, Toby was deeply concerned about Gerald's loss of appetite, and spared none of his culinary skills in producing dishes to tempt his jaded palate. All to no avail.

It was the day of decision and as he vigorously dusted the living room furniture, Toby wondered how David's crane had fared in the competition. The thought was still fresh in his mind, when a tap came on the front door and David walked in, carrying the suitcase he had borrowed from Toby. The expression on his face and the manner in which he quietly replaced the case, left no doubt in Toby's mind that his hopes of winning the competition had been dashed. Toby watched sympathetically as he waved a 'Thanks' with his hand and moved miserably back to the door.

"What won it then?" Toby asked.

David turned at the door.

"A radio-controlled tank."

Toby grunted his disapproval.

"Doesn't sound a patch on your crane," he said loyally.

David shrugged his shoulders dejectedly.

"It fired shells with simulated smoke."

Toby snorted disparagingly.

"I bet it couldn't pick up a car and put it on a transporter."

It would have been a strange tank if it had been capable of such a feat, but as far as Toby was concerned, logic went out of the window when it was a question of family loyalty.

David smiled, wanly, at his young brother's attempts to cheer him up. He waved half-heartedly and went out of the room, closing the door behind him.

Toby watched the door sadly and, as the sound of his brother's footsteps died away, picked up his duster and went through the motions of dusting the sideboard.

He had just finished the dusting and had flopped down on the sofa when the door burst open and Gerald breezed in and headed straight for the drinks cabinet.

"My God, what an afternoon!" he muttered as he poured himself a Scotch. "Six clients one after the other with exciting problems ranging from a dispute over who has to mend a partition fence to a possession order where all they're going to get is a moth-eaten carpet and some curtains that should have been thrown away years ago." As he knocked back his Scotch and put down the glass, he noticed Toby, looking very subdued, sitting on the sofa.

"You look about as happy as your brother," he said.

Toby looked up.

"Who?"

"David," Gerald replied, producing a screwdriver from his pocket and waving it at Toby. "I just went upstairs to borrow this. He's sitting there with a face as long as a fiddle." He moved back to the drinks cabinet and poured himself another Scotch as Toby asked:

"Where are all the others?"

"Gone to the cinema, I think he said," Gerald replied as he looked into the ice bucket. "No ice!" he exclaimed, picking up the ice bucket and taking it through into the kitchen. "He wouldn't tell me what's wrong," he called through the door, "but he looked as if the bottom has just fallen out of his world."

"It has," Toby muttered sadly to himself. "And that's why I'll have to pack my case." He got up from the sofa and met Gerald as he came in with his glass of Scotch from the kitchen.

"I'm very sorry, Mr Parish, but I shall have to move back upstairs," he said solemnly. "Now before you make any objections, I'm afraid I have to tell you that my decision is final."

Gerald could hardly believe his luck. He took a sip of his whisky and feigned dismay.

"Well, naturally I'm disappointed . . ."

Toby silenced him by putting up his hand and cutting right in on him.

"I am forced to take this course of action through circumstances beyond my control . . ." he went on in a fair imitation of Gerald at his most pompous ". . . and I'm equally sorry to have to tell you that you will have to make your own dinner tonight."

Gerald sighed with relief. At long last, he would be able to eat again. To taste real food for the first time since Toby commandeered his kitchen. It was a consummation devoutly to be wished.

"Well, that too is a bit of a blow, but I'll try to bear it," he smiled hypocritically, raising his glass to his lips.

Toby carried on talking as he moved around the room, picking up his belongings and throwing them into the suitcase.

"Of course I won't be deserting you altogether . . ." he went on, smiling reassuringly at Gerald. "I'll pop down from time to time to make sure you're okay. You know, check if there's any washing or ironing to be done, perhaps cook you a proper meal occasionally."

Gerald forced a smile to his lips as he replied, "That makes me feel a lot better about the whole thing."

Toby collected his hat and coat, picked up the suitcase and moved to the door.

"You don't have to think of it as goodbye, Mr Parish," he said as he opened the door. "We'll still be seeing a lot of each other, I promise you."

Gerald raised his glass in response and as Toby went through the door, he took a sip of whisky, settled back in his chair and raised his glass again to the closed door.

His face wreathed in smiles, he murmured philosophically, "Au revoir!"

Upstairs, David was alone in the flat, sitting at the dining table, staring dejectedly at the working model of the crane in front of him. He looked up as the door opened and Toby entered the room.

Toby dumped his case, together with his coat and hat, on the nearest chair, picked up a pack of cards from the writing desk, crossed over and sat down opposite David. He pushed the crane out of the way, dealt out five cards each, put down the pack and turned up the top card.

"I dealt. Your lead!" he said, looking over and watching his brother carefully.

After a moment's pause, David shrugged, smiled faintly and picked up his cards. As he began to sort the cards in his hand, he suddenly exclaimed, "Cheat!"

His belligerent expression softened as he looked across the table and saw Toby grinning happily back at him.

Chapter Eleven

Too Hot To Handle

Gerald was trying to watch the lunchtime news on the small portable television set on his desk, and at the same time carry on a telephone conversation with a rather slow-witted individual at the Planning Department. It was an exercise that was causing him a good deal of irritation.

"What about roads? New roads? Any of those planned for the future?" He listened as the official waffled out some excuse at the other end of the phone, and then blasted into the mouthpiece, "Well, if the map isn't in your office, I suggest you go and find the office it is in." He heaved a monumental sigh and groaned wearily. "Yes. I'll hold on." Holding the receiver away from his ear, he reached over and turned up the volume on the television set. A Detective Superintendent was sitting beside the newscaster on the screen.

"Five thousand pounds," the newscaster was saying. "That's the price put on a single piece of jewelry. A pendant to be exact, a large sapphire surrounded by diamonds."

Gerald watched idly as the newscaster went on. "Detective Superintendent Percival, here in the studio with me, has a special interest in it since it was stolen earlier today from this shop in the suburbs of Bristol."

Gerald recognised the shop from the 'still' that flashed up on the screen as being one of the most expensive jewellers in Bristol. The phone began to crackle in his hand, and as he put the receiver back to his ear, he reached forward and turned down the volume on the set. He listened as the planning official told him the results of his search.

"No roads. Good!" he replied, before going on, "Now, what about factories? Any of those planned in the vicinity?" He grimaced as he listened to the reply, and then snapped, irritably. "Well go and find out where that damned office is!" He leaned over to the television set and turned up the volume again. The picture on the screen had changed to a 'still' of the interior of the jewellers. The announcer's voice continued over the slide.

". . . The assistant who was showing a prospective buyer the pendant was suddenly taken ill. Several of the customers and other staff rushed to his aid . . ." The picture on the screen changed back to the studio and the newscaster and Detective Superintendent Percival came back into vision. ". . . and by the time everybody's attention came back to the pendant . . ." the announcer went on, "it was gone!" He turned to address Percival, "Superintendent! Was the shop very busy at the time?" he asked.

"Quite busy, yes . . . the Superintendent replied, "as you would expect at that time of day in that particular area."

There was a voice at the end of the telephone and Gerald turned down the volume again as he resumed his telephone conversation.

"No factories. Good!" he replied. "Well thank you, Mr Francis, you've been most helpful," he said sarcastically. "Even if it did take nearly twenty minutes to find out something that could and should have been ascertained in as many seconds." He slammed down the receiver, turned up the volume and leaned back in his chair to watch the rest of the news. The Superintendent was still talking.

". . . and as you can see, a very distinctive piece of jewelry. Of course, the thief may break it up and try to sell the stones separately, but, even so, that sapphire would still be very recognisable."

As the Superintendent finished, the camera moved back onto the newscaster, who took up the story.

"Well, you'll be pleased to know that the assistant who

was taken ill is in the care of Marstone Hospital and is recovering well.'' He went on to add, "Recovery is a word we'd also like to be able to use in the case of the sapphire and diamond pendant . . ." The colour photograph of the pendant flashed onto the screen as the announcer's voice continued, "Once again we ask for your help. The number is 107493 or call your local police station and of course, any information will be treated in complete confidence."

Gerald yawned wearily, switched off the set and called through to the outer office.

"Nesta!"

"Yes Mr Parish," her voice came back through the partition.

Gerald got up and went over to the connecting door.

"Did you buy that present for Joanna's birthday?"

Nesta had a roll of sellotape in her hand and was busily sealing a parcel on her desk.

"I'm just wrapping it up now," she replied.

He went into the outer office and looked curiously at the parcel.

"What did you get her?"

"A book on flowers," Nesta smiled. "Just like you asked me to."

"Do you think it will impress her?"

"Of course it will, Mr Parish," Nesta gushed. "It's a beautiful book. Nice shiny cover and everything."

Gerald took the parcel from her and weighed it in his hand.

"Happy birthday, Joanna!" he chuckled mysteriously and glanced slyly at Nesta. "Must keep the little baskets happy, mustn't we? Yes. At all costs."

The Lamperts' living room was a hive of activity as all the children and Adela busied themselves with the preparations for Joanna's birthday party.

Toby was blowing up balloons with a bicycle pump to which David had fitted an adapter, and though Toby's excessive enthusiasm to blow them up to their maximum size caused a high casualty rate in burst balloons, the number festooning the ceiling showed that he also had a lot of success.

The kitchen was absolutely littered with goodies in various stages of preparation, with Adela fussing around excitedly in Polish, preparing trifles, turning out jellies and grilling sausages and putting them on sticks.

The four older children were sitting around the dining table and had formed a sandwich-making assembly line, with Richard slicing, David buttering, Bill filling and Joanna cutting up the sandwiches and piling them up onto plates.

The arrangement was a good one, and with Adela working on her own in the kitchen, the problems the language barrier might have caused were all but eliminated. The only time it reared its head was when Bill called through to Adela:

"We're running out of corned beef and cheese!"

This brought a strong reaction from the au pair, who came storming out of the kitchen, shouting angrily.

"No, not running out!" she blazed. "You not running out!" She turned round to include the others. "You all not go nowhere! You stay here, help!"

Bill didn't try to explain or argue. He got up and was about to go to collect the things he needed when a knock came on the front door. Adela, still fuming with indignation, pushed past him and opening the door to reveal a smiling Gerald bearing a gift-wrapped parcel.

"Good day, Adela!" he beamed, speaking slowly and distinctly for her benefit. "Settling-in-all-right-are-you? Enjoying-your-stay-here?"

She stared blankly at him.

"Stay?"

"Stay-here," Gerald explained slowly.

Adela shook her head violently.

"No! Not possible," she gestured, wildly, in the direction of the kitchen. "Is getting everything ready for party," she said, turning on her heel and going back to the kitchen.

Gerald smiled after her, and then crossed over to hand

the present to Joanna.

"Happy birthday, Joanna!" he greeted her with studied sincerity.

She took it from him with an expression of surprised delight.

"Thank you very much, Mr Parish."

"My pleasure!" he beamed, as he watched her eagerly opening the package. "I think you'll find it very much up your street."

"Oh, thank you very much, Mr Parish!" Joanna said, as she unwrapped the book and looked through it hastily. "It's a pity it's about cut flowers, and I only like them when they're alive."

"Oh . . . oh, I see. Well now, what other presents have you had?"

"Well!" she began, and after a pause started to race through the catalogue of gifts she'd received from the rest of the family. "Mummy gave me a super new dress and Bill gave me a fantastic book on boxing and David . . ." she paused and looked anxiously at David as she tried to remember the name of the electronic device he had given her.

"A triple circuit, line, time-correlator and selection switch," David grinned across at her as she blankly nodded in agreement.

"He gave me one of those . . ." she went on, ". . . and Toby gave me a marvellous book on prehistoric monsters which was given to him last Christmas . . ."

"It's the thought that counts," Toby chipped in sourly.

"And Richard . . ." She pulled out a pendant which she had been wearing under her dress and thrust it under Gerald's nose, "Richard gave me this!"

Gerald hardly had time to register the sapphire and diamond pendant she showed him when there was a piercing scream from the kitchen and they all turned to see a distraught Adela, tearfully bewailing her grief over a grill tray of incinerated sausages. The poor girl's screeching set Gerald's teeth on edge and as the others rushed forward to console her, he slipped out through the door and made his way down the stairs to his office.

Once inside, he crossed over to behind his desk and slumped, wearily, into the chair. His eyes lit on the blank television screen on his desk and suddenly his memory clicked into gear. His eyes widened with horror as the picture clarified in his mind. He rose abruptly to his feet.

"That pendant!" he gasped, "My God!" He looked up at the portrait of his father and muttered through his teeth. "Not only is your eldest grandson a thug, but two down the line and you've got a jewel thief!" He stood for a moment, deep in thought, and then, suddenly, turned away and rushed out of his room, through the outer office and out to the hall.

When Gerald reached the front door to the upstairs flat, he didn't bother to knock. He swung the door open and strode straight into the room, crossed over to Joanna and without a word, took the pendant in his hand and examined it closely for some moments before letting it go. Then he turned to stare at Richard, who was still busily slicing bread.

"Richard!" He spoke with controlled fury in his voice.

Richard looked up innocently,

Gerald indicated the pendant Joanna was wearing.

"Do you realise half the country's police forces are looking for you?" he asked sternly.

Richard stared back at him, shrugged his shoulders and smiled non-committally. Gerald began to pace around the room like a caged animal as he went on.

"They've assigned a Detective Superintendent to the case. They've even had him on television!" As he continued to pace up and down, Richard got up from his chair and sighed wearily.

"Okay, if they're going to make that much fuss about it, I'll take it back."

Gerald stopped pacing and turned to face him.

"Sit down!" he snapped. Richard sat, and he went on, "You can't just take five thousand pounds' worth of jewelry back! They'll send you to reform school and throw away the key.''

Richard didn't seem at all concerned and just shrugged nonchalantly.

"So we'll keep it. That'll solve the problem.''

Gerald was getting quite exasperated as he tried to talk sense into the boy.

"Richard! The only way to solve the problem is for you to stop stealing things.''

Richard looked up at him disarmingly.

"But I only borrowed it,'' he said, simply.

Gerald clutched his head despairingly, then turned and grabbed Richard by the shoulders and looked him, imploringly, in the eyes.

"Steal! Steal! The word is steal!'' He was pleading, begging the boy to understand, but his words just didn't seem to register. He let go of his shoulders and put his hand to his head. "My God, you've really excelled yourself this time!''

Joanna fingered the pendant as it hung from her neck, her brow furrowed in concentration.

"Couldn't we get it back to the shop without anyone knowing who took it?'' she suggested. "Sort of slip it back when they're not looking?''

Bill nodded as he got up from the table.

"Yeah! Nothing to it!'' he said, extending his hand to Joanna. "Give me the pendant, Joanna!'' As she undid the fastening at the back of her neck, he turned and grinned confidently at Gerald. "I'll pop round there, now . . .''

Gerald cut in on him quickly.

"You're not popping anywhere!'' He moved over and took the pendant from Joanna. "The whole operation has to be thought out properly and carefully,'' he said, putting the pendant into his pocket. "You can't just walk into the shop and throw it onto the counter.''

"Why don't we post it?'' David suggested.

Gerald shook his head and waved aside the suggestion. "It might get lost.''

"Couldn't you register it?'' Richard asked.

Gerald rounded on him sharply.

"In whose name?" he snapped. As Richard deflated and turned away, Gerald sighed, biting his thumb as he wrestled with the problem. "I shall have to give it some thought, conceive the safest plan for returning the pendant and put it into operation as soon as possible." Still deep in thought, he turned, walked slowly over to the door and went out.

Joanna watched him go and after a moment's pause turned to Richard and sighed.

"Now you really have done it, Richard!"

He looked up at her with a pained expression in his eyes, shrugged and went back to his task of slicing the bread.

Chapter Twelve

The Alibi

It was time for the evening news, and Gerald had poured himself a Scotch and switched on the TV set on his desk. The introductory music faded out and the newscaster came up on the screen.

"Good evening!" the newscaster began. "Those of you who watched our midday edition of the news will have seen this photograph."

Gerald leaned forward in his chair as the colour photograph of the sapphire and diamond pendant flashed up on the screen.

The newscaster's voice continued.

"Stolen earlier this morning, it was mysteriously returned late this afternoon to the jeweller's shop from which it was stolen."

Gerald began to get nervous when the camera went back to the studio where Detective Superintendent Percival was sitting beside the newscaster, who was interviewing him.

"Superintendent! You have a theory about all this?" he asked.

"It seems very clear to me . . ." the Superintendent began, ". . . that the thief got cold feet. When he realised the value of the jewelry he'd stolen, quite possibly having seen your programme earlier today, he knew he had no chance of fencing it, of selling it." The Superintendent shrugged. "It was too hot for him to handle, so . . . he returned it."

"Now is that the end of the case?" the newscaster asked. "Will the police now drop their investigations?"

"Certainly not!" the Superintendent retorted. "The

law has been broken. A crime has been committed and the man responsible has got to be found!''

"You said man,'' the newscaster probed. "The man responsible has got to be found?''

Percival nodded.

"Like all petty crooks, they slip up some time or another.'' A faint smile crossed his face. "A witness saw him replacing the pendant. Called us and gave us a very good description.''

Gerald almost choked on his Scotch as an identikit picture flashed up on the screen. It bore a remarkable resemblance to himself, and he felt sure that any of his acquaintances would recognise him from it. He rose ashen-faced from the chair as the announcer continued.

"And there it is! If anybody recognises this man, the number again is 107293 or your local police station and . . . as always, your information will be treated in the utmost confidence . . . and now over to Peter Lewis for more of today's news . . .''

Gerald reached forward and switched off the set, drained the rest of his Scotch in one gulp, and rushed out through the door.

The party was in full swing upstairs and the noise drifting out to the hall and stairs was quite deafening as Gerald made his way up through the foliage. He went straight into the flat, closed the door behind him and stood for a moment, anxiously peering over the multitude of children's heads bobbing around in the living room. The Lampert children were all dancing, as were most of the neighbourhood children, to the current pop tunes blaring out of David's hifi speakers; others stood around in groups watching the dancers and swaying to the rhythm as they tucked into the plentiful supplies of sausages on sticks, sandwiches, trifles, jellies and pop that burdened the trestle table at the side.

Gerald suddenly spotted Mary, took his courage in both hands, and began to manoeuvre his way through the stamping, gyrating, hand-clapping youngsters to the

89

kitchen, where Mary and Adela were busily organizing replenishments for the food and drink supply.

"Looks like everyone's having a good time!" he gasped, as he finally made it to the kitchen.

Mary nodded breathlessly.

"Look Mary!" he said. "Could we possibly go and talk somewhere a little quieter perhaps? My office?"

She was loading bottles onto a tray.

"It's a little difficult just now, Gerald," she replied, indicating the crowds of children in the living room.

"The thing is . . . it's er . . . rather important . . ." Gerald persisted, as she picked up the tray and started to make her way across the kitchen. He trailed after her and tried to impress on her the urgency of the situation. ". . . You see, we all decided . . . that is the kids and I decided that we wouldn't bother you with Richard's latest little exploit, but it has now become rather complicated, to say the least."

She turned to face him at the mention of Richard's name.

"Oh no!" she gasped. "What's he done this time?"

Gerald paused and looked around to make sure no one was in earshot before replying.

"He stole five thousand pounds' worth of jewelry!"

She stood for a moment, transfixed with horror, then looked down at the tray in her hand.

"I'll just get rid of this."

He followed her out, and after she'd deposited the trayful of lemonade on the buffet table, they threaded their way through the dancing children, out through the front door and down the stairs to his office.

The intense shock Mary experienced as Gerald related the whole sorry story of the theft of the sapphire and diamond pendant, seemed to drain her of all feeling. Then, as her numbed senses came back to life, her adrenalin-charged protective instinct took over and, strangely, stretched out to envelop not only her tight-knit family, but the man she'd so recently regarded as her enemy, slumped down in the chair. She paced, restlessly, as she racked her brain for a solution to what was the worst problem she'd ever had to wrestle with.

"Do you think anyone will recognise you from the identikit picture?"

"I recognised me," Gerald smiled, wryly.

She stood for a moment in agonized thought, then heaved a great sigh and made the only decision she could make.

"Well, I'll just have to tell the police it was Richard and . . ."

Gerald leaped to his feet and cut across her firmly.

"No! You can't do that!"

She was surprised by the vehemence of his reaction and for a moment, a hope flickered in her breast that it might be possible to avoid informing the police. But what else could she do when the only other alternative would leave Gerald to take the blame?

"We don't have any alternative!" she said flatly.

Gerald turned to face her and talked earnestly.

"Look!" he reasoned. "Typewriters, lawnmowers and the other bits and pieces he's been borrowing on and off . . ." He dismissed them in an expansive gesture. "That's one thing." He paused for a moment before continuing. "An antique, unique, rare sapphire and diamond pendant is quite another. They'll throw the proverbial book at him. Richard will have to go to court, and once they find out, as they will, that he's been 'borrowing' things from around the neighbourhood for God knows how long, you can be sure they'll insist he goes into care."

Mary slumped into a chair as the full implication of Gerald's words sank home.

"All right, let's take it stage by stage," Gerald began, looking intently at Mary. "One, we cannot, under any circumstances, let Richard get involved in this." As she began to protest that Richard was already involved, he put his hand out to silence her and went on. "Two. I am already involved in it up to my neck and I have to get out of it. Three. To do that I need an alibi. Four. Since you were at work, the only alibi I can possibly establish is that I was with that bunch of maniacs of yours upstairs when I was supposed to be returning the jewelry."

Mary stood up abruptly.

"That's it!" she exclaimed. "That bunch of maniacs of mine upstairs are the best 'liars' I've ever come across." Gerald looked across the desk anxiously, fearing his remarks offended her. As their eyes met, she smiled wryly, reassuring him. "I can personally vouch for that."

His relief was evident as he smiled, understandingly, back at her. He got up from his chair, crossed over to the drinks cabinet and poured out two large brandies.

"I think you could do with this!" he smiled, as he handed a drink to her.

"We'll have to brief the children," Mary thought things through. "You were 'helping with the preparations for the party all afternoon'. We must drum that into Toby's head, especially: his heart's in the right place, but his mind sometimes wanders."

They raised their glasses to each other.

"To unavoidable subterfuge!" Mary joked conspiratorially.

"I couldn't have put it better myself," Gerald reflected as they drank.

Chapter Thirteen

The Best Laid Plans

It was the morning after the party and Toby, in dressing-gown and slippers, was going down to the front door to collect the milk from the step. As he bent down to pick up the bottles, he froze as he saw two large, highly polished boots on the step beside the milk bottles. He stood up and stared up into the face of Detective Superintendent Percival. Remembering his briefing of the night before, he was relieved by the fact that the man was dressed in civilian clothes, and not in police uniform as he feared.

"Morning!" he greeted him brightly.

The Superintendent smiled down at him.

"Good morning. Is your mother in?"

Toby shook his head.

"She's gone to work," he replied as he turned to go back into the hall, stopping in his tracks as the Superintendent added, "Well actually, I was looking for a Mr Gerald Parish!"

Toby turned back to face him and nodded down the hall.

"Down there! If you've got an appointment with him, you're a bit early. He never gets to his office before about nine o'clock." He started to go up the stairs and called back over his shoulder, "If then!"

Percival had followed him into the hall.

"Yes, well. I don't have an appointment, as such."

"Oh, but you must have!" Toby replied as he began once again to make his way up the stairs. "Mr Parish only sees people by appointment. He's a solicitor, you know!"

"Yes, I'm aware of that." Percival chuckled, pleasantly. "And for your information, young man, the police don't need appointments."

Toby stopped suddenly and turned to stare incredulously at the big man smiling up at him from the hall.

"You're not the police!" he said. "Where's your uniform?"

The Detective Superintendent seemed a little irked by the cheeky young lad's scepticism and snapped rather shortly, "I happen to be a detective!" Then, feeling a little annoyed with himself for allowing a little boy to upset him, he softened and asked smilingly, "Would you like to see my badge?"

The penny dropped instantly and Toby began to get interested.

"What? Like Kojak?" he gasped.

"Something like that," the superintendent grinned.

Toby began to move back down the stairs. He'd never seen a real live detective before, and he was intrigued to find himself face to face with one. At the same time, he remembered what his mother had told him and he determined to play it cool, and put him right off the scent — just like they did on the telly.

"Well, in that case, I can save you a bit of trouble," he said, putting the milk bottles down on the bottom stair. "You don't need to bother to see Mr Parish because I can tell you that he was here at the time."

The Superintendent looked at him quizzically.

"Here?"

"Well!" Toby shrugged, "Upstairs with us. He was helping us get everything ready for the party."

Percival was still puzzled.

"When?" he asked.

"Yesterday. When you think he was somewhere else," Toby replied.

The detective looked at him suspiciously as he began to smell an alibi.

"Ah, and where would that somewhere else be, exactly?"

Toby eyed him cautiously and thought carefully before he answered. He was far too smart to fall into that trap.

"Wherever it is you think he was," he replied.

Percival was getting decidedly interested and beginning to feel that he was really onto something.

"I haven't said he was anywhere else," he said, looking intently at Toby.

Toby shrugged, climbed a couple of stairs to get on level terms with the Superintendent, turned and smiled disarmingly back at him.

"No, you haven't, have you?"

The boy's attitude was a little disconcerting, and Percival was getting a little confused.

"This er . . . this somewhere else," he began to fish, haltingly. "It wouldn't be a certain jeweller's shop, would it? The one down the road, for instance?"

"I don't know," Toby replied, practically. "You're the one who's saying Mr Parish was somewhere else, so you're the one who must know where he was."

The detective seemed to be getting nowhere fast. At the same time he was convinced that the boy knew something and that if he continued to play it along, would sooner or later make a slip.

"Right!" he smiled patiently. "I'm saying it was the jeweller's shop down the road."

Toby shook his head.

"Impossible. He was here at the time."

"At what time?"

The Superintendent was trying to rush him into making a mistake, but Toby wasn't going to be caught out that way. It was becoming a game to him, and he was really beginning to enjoy himself.

"At the time you think he was at the jeweller's shop," he smirked.

Percival paused for a moment before trying a new tack. He spoke slowly, almost ponderously.

"If . . . I repeat, if he was in the jeweller's shop, what might he have been doing there?"

"That's easy," Toby replied, smugly. He already had the answer, pat, in his mind, and was not at all thrown when the detective pressed, eagerly.

"What then? What?"

He was savouring his moment of victory and smiled condescendingly at Percival before delivering the line that would send him retreating in confusion, just like they did on the telly.

"Whatever it is you think he was doing there," he drawled, smiling through half-closed eyes at the detective, who was rapidly losing his temper.

"I don't think he was doing anything!" Percival snapped testily.

"Good!" Toby replied calmly, as he picked up the milk bottles and started to go back up the stairs. "Well, I hope I've been of some help."

"You've been no damned help whatsoever!" Percival snorted furiously.

Toby turned on the stairs to face him, reprovingly.

"There's no need to shout!"

Percival choked back the desire to put the cheeky young brat over his knee and give him the spanking he deserved, but somehow he managed to calm down and force an apology to his lips.

"I'm sorry. I apologise," he said.

"That's quite all right!" Toby was pleased with the way he'd handled the detective, and, in the flush of victory, couldn't resist the temptation to press on and consolidate his advantage. "As I said, there's no need to see Mr Parish now because I've explained everything."

"Well!" Percival shrugged, disarmingly. "I might just have a word with him, as I'm here."

Toby looked at him, sighed and smilingly shook his head.

"It's up to you," he said, in a tone that implied he was wasting his time. "But I can assure you he was here when you think he was at the jeweller's shop returning the pendant." As he moved on up the stairs, Toby suddenly realised that he'd pushed his luck a bit too far. He stopped and looked back at the Superintendent, stammering hopefully, "You did mention the pendant, didn't you?"

Percival was shaking his head, deliberately, a triumphant smile on his face.

"No," he said slowly, "but you did!"

Utterly deflated, Toby turned and began to move disconsolately up the stairs just as the door to Gerald's flat
opened, and Gerald emerged, humming happily to
himself. He closed the door behind him and was crossing
the hall to his office when he caught sight of the Detective
Superintendent at the foot of the stairs. He stopped
humming and greeted him cheerfully.

"Good morning! Can I be of any help?"

"If you're Gerald Parish, you can be of immense help,"
Percival replied.

"Yes. I am Gerald Parish," he smiled and looked
questioningly at the Superintendent, who responded by
identifying himself.

"Detective Superintendent Percival!"

The introduction was hardly necessary, but Gerald
played it coolly and stared blankly back at Percival as
though he'd never heard of him. The detective eyed him
carefully, produced the identikit picture from his pocket
and handed it to Gerald.

"A remarkable likeness, I think you'll agree," he said,
as he watched for Gerald's reaction.

Confident in the cast-iron alibi he'd created, Gerald
glanced at the picture and handed it back to Percival.

"As you say, remarkable," he smiled, then instantly
adopting a no-nonsense, down-to-business attitude,
asked, "Now! What can I do for you?"

The Superintendent wasted no time on niceties, but got
straight down to the nitty gritty of the matter in hand.

"You could tell me why you were returning five thousand
pounds' worth of sapphire and diamond pendant to the
jeweller's shop up the road at approximately five o'clock
yesterday afternoon."

Gerald's face took on a pained expression of wronged
innocence as he exclaimed, "Terribly sorry to disappoint
you, Superintendent, but I was . . ." He glanced up the
stairs and saw Toby for the first time. "Ah! Well there
you are. Young Toby here can vouch for the fact that I
was . . ."

"Yes, yes!" Percival interrupted. "Young Toby has already told me all about your alibi." He chuckled to himself as he glanced at Gerald. "Sounded a bit thin, I'm afraid."

For the first time, Gerald was beginning to feel anxious, but tried, desperately, not to show it. He looked up the stairs to Toby.

"Toby, er . . . what exactly did you tell Superintendent Percival?" he asked.

Toby shuffled, miserably, on the stairs.

"I told him about you not returning the pendant and he hadn't said anything about a pendant," he mumbled, guiltily.

Gerald recovered with remarkable resilience.

"Well, of course he knew about the pendant!" He glanced up the stairs to Toby. "You saw it on television, didn't you Toby?" There was no response and he turned to glare at the blank, unhappy face staring back at him down the stairs. "Yes you did," he insisted. "You remember. We were all watching the news programme and we saw Superintendent Percival and they showed us a photograph of the pendant!" He turned to Percival and laughed, nervously. "I'm surprised neither of us recognised you." There was an amused twinkle in the Superintendent's eye as Gerald turned to him and asked, "Well! Is there anything else I can do for you, Superintendent?"

Percival nodded his head.

"Yes. You can accompany me to the Police Station for further questioning!" He smiled grimly.

Toby watched anxiously from the stairs as Gerald stared incredulously at Percival and exclaimed,

"Superintendent! Are you honestly trying to tell me that you believe that I stole that pendant?"

Percival shook his head.

"No," he replied, going on to trample right through Gerald's outraged protestations. "What I do believe is that you know who did steal it, because I know, as sure as eggs are eggs, that it was you who took it back to the jeweller's shop.''

Gerald tried to bluster his way out, getting on his high horse, rounding on the detective and pulling the rank of his profession.

"Now you listen to me, Superintendent!" he blazed high-handedly. "Let me remind you that I am a solicitor and I know my rights!"

Completely unmoved by his outburst, Percival replied, "Good! Then you will also know that, unless you agree to accompany me to the Police Station to answer our questions, I can arrest you and take you there to be charged."

Toby, listening over the bannisters, gasped in astonishment as he began to realise the seriousness of Gerald's predicament. He listened with bated breath as Gerald continued to fight.

"I've never heard of anything so ridiculous in my life!" he raged. "Charged with what? Eh? Tell me what!" he challenged the Superintendent. "Charged with what?"

Percival waited patiently for Gerald to finish, before replying calmly.

"Attempting to pervert the course of justice, obstructing the police in the performance of their duties, harbouring an offender, aiding and abetting after the event, not to mention handling stolen goods." He smiled smugly at Gerald. "Enough?" he asked.

As he listened to the catalogue of charges that could be preferred against Gerald, Toby tried to imagine how many years he'd have to spend in gaol. Feeling guiltier than ever, he turned and disappeared quickly up the stairs.

Gerald was really incensed, as he stormed back at the Superintendent.

"This is preposterous," he raged. "You haven't a grain of evidence to support any of those charges!" He turned to bait the detective with a question, "What have you got? Eh? I ask you!"

There was no response from Percival and he made a broad gesture signifying nothing. "You have an identikit picture that vaguely resembles a description of me given to you by some snotty-nosed little girl, and that's about the sum of it! As a Solicitor at Law, I have to inform you that on the evidence you have presented so far, you haven't got a dog's chance of getting me convicted of not mowing my front lawn, let alone being involved with stolen jewelry.''

Percival nodded his head in agreement.

"Correct!" he conceded. Then after a long pause he turned and smiled grimly, adding, "Until now!" As Gerald pondered on the significance of his remark, Percival mused, "Snotty-nosed little girl!" Then he turned to ask Gerald, "How did you know it was a little girl who gave us your description?"

Taken completely off his guard, Gerald floundered. "On the television. You said . . ."

"Never!" Percival cut in. "Deliberately didn't mention the little girl. But one thing I always do is to have those newscasts recorded . . ." he smiled magnanimously at Gerald, ". . . so we can play it back to the court if you so wish." As Gerald stared unbelievingly at him, the Superintendent continued to enjoy his moment of triumph to the full. "But you said it!" he went on, wagging his finger at Gerald. "Snotty-nosed little girl! The only way you could have known that, is because you were returning the jewelry yourself." Loving every minute of the game, he smiled. "So it was you, sir, wasn't it?"

Gerald didn't reply. He just continued to stare back at him in utter dejection.

Having had his fun, Percival started to get down to the serious business of the case — the apprehension of the thief. He stood for a moment in thought, then turned to Gerald, who still seemed in a state of shock.

"All right sir!" he began. "I'm going to pay you the courtesy of accepting that you personally didn't steal the pendant. So you're covering for someone. Now! Who is it?" He waited for some moments, and when there was no response from Gerald, snapped impatiently. "I'll ask you again. Who took that pendant?"

A voice rang out from among the greenery.

"I did."

Gerald and the Superintendent turned sharply, to see Richard coming down the stairs. Percival put his hand to his head and sighed.

"My God, there's another of them!" He looked directly up at Richard. "All right, sonny. You and who I can only assume is your brother have done your bit for today." He turned back to Gerald and asked. "What do you do? Supplement their pocket money or something?" He put his hand on Gerald's shoulder and sighed wearily. "Come on, let's go down to the station."

Richard moved quickly down into the hallway and went straight up to the Superintendent.

"Mr Parish took the pendant back, but it was me who borrowed it in the first place," he protested. "You can't arrest him. You can't send him to prison!"

Gerald tried to quieten him.

"I appreciate your concern, Richard. Now you go back upstairs, will you."

The boy was not to be silenced, and moved round to look Percival directly in the eye.

"Why don't you listen to me?" he pleaded. "I borrowed the pendant!"

Percival pushed his way past him and opened the front door as Richard continued to shout, desperately.

"It's true! I borrowed it! It was me! I borrowed it!"

The Superintendent continued to ignore his impassioned pleas and motioned Gerald to precede him through the door. As Gerald went out and Percival followed him through the door, Richard rushed to the door, screaming.

"It was me! All right, I stole it! I stole it! I stole it!"

As Percival started to close the door, Richard took a ring from his pocket and thrust it under his nose. "I stole this ring at the same time!" he sobbed.

The Superintendent stopped suddenly, pushed the door open again and looked at the ring in the boy's hand.

"There was a ring missing!" he recollected, taking the ring from Richard and looking at it closely. He sighed heavily and after a moment's hesitation preceded Gerald back into the house.

Chapter Fourteen

Hope and Despair

The Lampert household was unusually quiet and the expressions on the faces of the four children that remained there suggested that the End of the World might well be imminent. Bill, Joanna, David and Toby were all there in the living room, sitting silently in an atmosphere that seemed heavily charged with impending doom. Even Adela, who had only a vague idea of what had happened, was affected by the gloom, but, practical person that she was, sought to use the situation to improve her English. She had her dictionary in her hand as she approached David.

"Your brother, Richard?" she laboured haltingly. "He go to prison?"

David sighed and glanced round at the others before he replied.

"We don't know yet."

Adela beamed all over her face.

"No!" she exclaimed, delightedly.

"Don't know . . . know." He was in a highly nervous state and the irritation showed in his voice as he tried to explain.

"We're waiting to find out."

Her face clouded.

"I not understand." She looked, blankly, at David.

"He might go to prison," he replied, shortly.

The poor girl was more confused than ever and thumbed, frantically, through the pages of her dictionary to find the word 'might'.

"Might . . ." she frowned, then as her eyes lit upon the word, her confusion increased as she went on to read the definition given. "It say strength!" she exclaimed as she looked appealingly to David for help.

He was spared from the daunting task of explaining the several uses of the word by the sudden arrival of their mother, Richard and Gerald. The children all leaped to their feet as the front door opened and they came into the room. Fearing the worst, none of the children could bring themselves to ask after the result of the hearing. They just stood and stared, and it was Gerald who put them out of their suspense.

"Fined fifty pounds and put on probation for one year," he announced as he moved over to them, going on to say, "Which means he has to report to me once a week, when I will make him do odd jobs to pay off the fifty pounds I've just lent him to pay the fine."

There was an excited yelp from Toby, who ran straight over and flung his arms round Gerald, while the others gathered around, babbling excitedly.

"Mr Parish. You're brilliant!" David enthused unstintingly, as the other children eagerly nodded their agreement.

"David, I'm forced to agree with you," Gerald replied lightly, thoroughly enjoying his unaccustomed popularity. "I'm also generous!" he laughed as he added, "I'm also waiving my fees."

"But how did you do it?" Bill asked. "We all thought they'd make Richard go to a Reform School or something."

Gerald was at his most flippant.

"Very simple really!" he replied. "I baffled them with my brilliant legal mind, stirred them with my oratory . . . and bribed the magistrate." As the children's spontaneous laughter subsided, he nodded over to Richard and spoke seriously. "In point of fact, Richard saved himself from being sent away. It was the psychiatrist's report that really swung the balance. He was impressed that Richard had made some progress."

"Progress!" Toby gasped, unbelievingly. "Nicking a sapphire and diamond pendant is progress?"

Joanna was still sceptical about Richard's progress.

"Oh, he only borrowed it," she said, sarcastically. "Didn't you, Richard?"

David and Bill laughed as they looked over at Richard and waited for him to agree with Joanna. Their expressions changed when, after several seconds, there was no response from him, and as they turned to Joanna and Toby it was clear from their blank looks of amazement, that they too shared their incredulity. They all looked back at Richard, who was standing, shamefacedly looking down at his feet.

The silence was broken when Mary suddenly exclaimed.

"All right, lunch! David and Richard, lay the table! Bill, peel the potatoes! Joanna, you help Adela with the cooking!" She turned to Toby. "And you, Toby, just keep out of everybody's way!"

As the children dispersed to their various tasks, she turned to Gerald.

"Mr Parish," she said with feeling. "How can I ever thank you?"

"Well, you could start by calling me Gerald," he smiled. "And secondly, there's a little favour I'm going to ask you to do for me."

"Just ask."

"Well," he began a little nervously, "I thought that I might take you out to lunch. There's an excellent restaurant . . ."

Mary suddenly remembered something and gasped. "Oh no . . ."

". . . not far from here . . ." Gerald continued, ". . . and over lunch, I will describe precisely what it is . . ."

Mary glanced at her watch and cut in, anxiously.

"Thank heavens you reminded me! What with the court case and everything, I'd clean forgotten that I'm having lunch with John." Preoccupied with her lunch date, she started to move to the stairs, then, remembering Gerald, turned back to him. "It was very kind of you to ask me to lunch and I really do owe you an enormous favour . . ." she raced on, "but I have to get changed and leave in . . ." she glanced at her watch again, "Good Lord!

I should have left ten minutes ago!''

Gerald watched, with ill-concealed disappointment, as she turned and dashed up the stairs, then turned to Toby, who had just wandered into the room.

''Who's John?'' he asked.

''Some bloke,'' Toby shrugged.

''What kind of bloke?'' Gerald asked anxiously. ''An uncle or somebody?''

Toby shook his head.

''Somebody Mummy met at work,'' he replied, glancing over to Bill and Richard, who were laying the table. ''Bill says he fancies her.''

''Does he?'' Gerald asked with growing concern.

Both Bill and Richard nodded their agreement.

''Mummy's always going out with him,'' Richard said as he crossed over to Gerald, adding confidentially, ''I don't think it's going to be long before we have a new daddy.''

Gerald stared back at him, struggling to overcome the tremendous shock he'd just received. He put his hand to his head.

''Oh my God!'' he groaned.

Chapter Fifteen

The Enemy at the Door

Gerald had had a restless night, struggling with the seemingly insurmountable problems that somehow had to be settled before his father's arrival. A new factor had arisen in the shape of John Purvis, and if the old Judge got wind of the fact that his 'daughter-in-law' had a regular boy-friend, it was going to take a lot of explaining away. He had wrestled with it for most the night, sleeping only in short snatches when his drooping eyelids just refused to stay open. His shortage of sleep showed in his red-rimmed eyes as he went down the hall to collect his mail next morning. He had opened the inner door and was taking his letters from the box when he heard the sound of children chattering as they came down the stairs.

As he got back into the hall, they were all bounding down the last flight, talking excitedly as they ran the gauntlet of plant pots and trailing greenery down the stairs. As soon as they saw Gerald, they made a bee-line for him and vied with each other to be first to tell him their exciting news.

"Mr Purvis is taking us out for the day. On the river!" Richard enthused.

"On a boat!" Toby yelled excitedly, pushing himself in front of Richard.

"What else would we be going on, you nit!" Bill scoffed at his young brother, as David cut in and announced:

"We're going to have a picnic!"

"And I'm going to catch some fish!" Toby declared, optimistically waving a primitive, home-made rod and line in Gerald's face.

"Then this evening," Joanna cut in, excitedly, "Mr Purvis is taking us all out to dinner."

"Sounds absolutely wonderful," Gerald replied without enthusiasm, just as Mary and Purvis came down into the hall. She moved straight across to him.

"Good morning Mr er . . . Gerald," she smiled as she corrected herself, and pointed in the direction of Purvis who was at her side. "This is John Purvis."

Gerald forced his taut features into a smile as he took the hand that was extended towards him and, from behind the mask, looked coldly at the stranger he regarded as his enemy. He was a man probably in his forties; well dressed, opulent-looking. The sort of smoothy women might regard as attractive. More than that, he was a damned nuisance and had to be eliminated from the scene if Gerald's plans were to be fulfilled.

"Very pleased to meet you," Purvis greeted him.

"Likewise," Gerald leered back, as diabolical schemes to dispose of his rival raced through his mind.

"You're a solicitor, then?" Purvis said, in an obvious attempt to make conversation.

"Yes," Gerald replied automatically as Purvis went on.

"In biscuits myself. Got a factory just outside Manchester. Purvis's chocolate-coated digestives is one of our specialities. You've probably heard of us?"

Gerald nodded, without taking his eyes off Purvis, and forced his features into a congratulatory smile.

"Often seen you on the supermarket shelves."

Purvis looked around, uncertainly, for a moment, then, as his eyes met Gerald's, the two men laughed, awkwardly, mirthlessly together. As the laughter petered out, Purvis moved to join the children, who were already kicking their heels impatiently around the open front door. Gerald followed him to the step, glanced up at the sky and smiled as he purred maliciously.

"Well, it looks like a bit of rain, doesn't it?"

Purvis glanced uncertainly at Mary before turning back to Gerald and replying without conviction:

"I'm usually lucky with the weather." He took Mary's

arm and, as they turned to go, took his leave of Gerald.
"Well, see you soon . . ."

Gerald watched them go, and as he stepped back into
the hall, the forced smile had gone from his face. He
closed the door behind him and scowled.

"Not if I see you first . . ."

He stood for a moment, seething with anger and frustration, muttered, "That man has got to go!", then turned
on his heel and went back to his office.

The telephone was ringing in Gerald's office. Nesta clicked
her teeth impatiently and hurriedly finished the complicated row she was doing before putting down her
knitting and picking up the receiver.

"Hello!" she cooed. "This is Gerald Parish's office."
She recoiled slightly as a voice snapped in her ear.

"Gerald!"

"I beg your pardon." She heard a heavy sigh from the
other end of the line before the voice growled, impatiently:

"Gerald Parish?"

"Yes, this is his office."

"I know it's his office!" the voice boomed. "You
informed me of that ten seconds ago. Just put him on
the line!"

Nesta bridled and quivered indignantly as she replied,
"Who is it calling please?"

"His father!" The voice snorted. "The same father
who's called him six times before!"

Her dander was up and she retorted, acidly, "Just
observing protocol. Hold the line please." She paused
as she rang the bell in Gerald's office, and as he lifted up
the receiver, went on, "Your father on the line, Mr Parish.
Do you wish to speak with him?"

"Of course he wishes to speak to me!" the old Judge
thundered. "Get off the line!"

Nesta was furious, and determined to have the last
word.

"Putting you through now," she said, icily, as she

switched the call through and firmly replaced the receiver on its rest.

Through the door in Gerald's office, he was exuding friendship and good will into the mouthpiece.

"Hello sir!" he greeted him. "How's the weather out there?"

"Same as it is where you are," came the gruff reply. "I'm in England."

Gerald stiffened and stared at the receiver in his hand. He didn't want to believe what he'd heard, and hoped against hope that his ears had deceived him. The blood drained from his cheeks as he gasped, "England!"

"I'm spending some time with my lawyers." The old Judge went on to outline his itinerary with total disregard for his son's feelings. "I'll be here for a few days sorting out my affairs. Tomorrow night, however, I shall dine with you and your family. Seven o'clock sharp!"

The adrenalin began to course through Gerald's veins as he racked his brains, thinking up a plausible excuse for cancelling the arrangement, stammering into the phone as he played for time.

"But you weren't due to arrive until er . . . until er . . ."

"For heaven's sake, Gerald!" old Henry blasted, almost shattering his son's eardrums. "You're still babbling like a neurotic schoolgirl." He repeated his direction. "Dinner. With your family. Seven o'clock sharp, tomorrow night!"

It was later that morning and Gerald was still at his desk, when the communicating door edged open and a ferrity head peered round into the room.

"Ah! Come in, Harold!" Gerald cried, putting aside the file he'd been working on, and indicating the chair at the other side of the desk.

Harold Searl pushed the door open, just wide enough to admit the rest of his body, sidled into the room and closed the door firmly behind him. He was a seedily dressed little man in his middle fifties, and his clothes clung to his sparse frame like damp sackcloth. His movements were quick and erratic, and his eyes shifted nervously, constantly flickering from right to left, up and down and back again.

"What is it this time, Mr Parish?" he asked, taking a quick glance over his shoulder and moving jerkily over to the chair. "Another writ to serve, is it?" He slumped down in the chair opposite Gerald and sighed, wheezily, "My God, I get all the excitement!"

"You get paid!"

"Yeah, but the fun's gone out of being a private detective ever since they changed the law." He fidgeted into a more comfortable position on the chair as he reminisced about the halcyon days of the private eye. "Remember the good old days? Nice juicy divorce cases, concealed tape recorders . . ." He stopped abruptly, his eyes scanning the moulding on the ceiling as his hands stealthily searched the underside of the desk for bugs. His gaze wobbled back to Gerald and his eyelids flickered as he sighed nostalgically, "radio-controlled, infra-red cameras . . . that sort of thing."

Gerald waited for him to stop babbling, took a deep breath and fixed him steadily with his eyes.

"I want you to investigate a John Purvis," he said, emphasising every word to impress on Harold the importance of the assignment.

The sleuth didn't seem particularly impressed.

"What's he done?" he leered, and without waiting for a reply went on, "Go on, tell me I've got the big one at last. Robbery with violence? Arson? Murder?"

Gerald ignored his heavy-handed attempt at humour as he continued with his briefing.

"All I've been able to find out about him so far is that he owns a large factory up north."

Harold was in irrepressible form and was playing for laughs.

"Making arms and shipping them illegally to the IRA, right?" he quipped.

Gerald was not amused by Harold's patter, and his irritation showed as he snapped back testily, "They make biscuits!"

110

"What's he planning to do?" Harold wheezed sarcastically. "Assassinate the Managing Director of Peek Freans?"

Gerald raised his voice and glared at the grubby little man leering across the desk.

"Your job is to find out everything you can about him," he blazed, and as Harold twitched nervously forward in his seat, continued more quietly. "There may be a skeleton in the cupboard somewhere. If there is, I want to know about it."

Harold was a little subdued as he sulked.

"Haven't given me much to go on, have you?"

"That's all I know!" Gerald snorted, almost taking the little man's head off. "Now will you get your proverbial 'up north' and find out a lot more. That's what I'm paying you for."

"A lot more of what?" the much chastened Harold asked. "What do you want to know about this bloke?"

A demonic gleam came into Gerald's eyes.

"Dirt!" he hissed. "I need dirt to throw at our Mr Purvis and I need it fast!"

The private eye nodded understandingly and his upper lip twitched up into a twisted, knowing smile. He got up from his chair, moved jerkily over to the door, and with a sly wink at Gerald slipped out through the door to perform his nefarious task.

Chapter Sixteen

The Skeleton in the Cupboard

When Gerald reached the Lamperts' living-room, he found the children squabbling over a train-set Mr Purvis had bought them. Mary was quietening them down, and as she turned from the children, she came face to face with Gerald. "Hello Gerald!" she smiled.

Gerald smiled nervously as he responded.

"Hello . . ." He cleared his throat as he tried to frame the proposition he was about to make. "I was wondering... that is to say . . ." Mary was looking at him curiously as he groped for the right words to gain her co-operation. Suddenly an idea came to him. "Well, as a matter of fact, it just happens to be my birthday today," he lied glibly.

"Oh . . . well, many happy returns of the day!" Mary exclaimed, turning to the children and announcing, "Children! It's Mr Parish's birthday today."

He waited, a little shamefacedly, for the chorus of 'Happy Birthdays' to subside, then he turned to include the children.

"Thank you!" he smiled, going on a little anxiously to say, "Actually, the only reason I mentioned it was because . . . well, because I'd like you to come to a light supper this evening. A sort of celebration, a birthday party so to speak." He experienced some misgiving as he glanced round at the children, whose faces displayed little enthusiasm for his suggestion.

Mary was more considerate.

"That is really very kind of you, Gerald," she replied, and casting a reproving look at the children, went on, "Well of course we would all love to come to supper with you, but it can't be too late. The children have to get to bed."

"Seven o'clock?" Gerald suggested, eager to be accommodating. Mary glanced back at the glum faces of the children again and refusing to be influenced by them, turned back to Gerald.

"Yes. Seven o'clock will be fine."

Gerald smiled with relief at the success of his little ploy.

"Good!" he exclaimed. "Well, see you all later." He drew Mary to one side and spoke quietly. "Something we must discuss before . . ." He looked back at the children who were all straining their ears to listen. He moved over to the door, opened it and called back over his shoulder. "Oh, by the way, Adela's invited as well, of course." He beamed an ingratiating smile and went out through the door.

As the door closed behind him, a loud groan went up from the children. Mary rounded on them sharply.

"You're all being very unfair to Mr Parish," she admonished them. "I know we've had problems with him in the past," she conceded, "but just recently, he has really been making a big effort to be nice."

"Can't Mr Purvis come as well?" Richard pleaded. "At least he's a bit of fun."

There was an excited hubbub from the rest of the children, who clearly went along with Richard's suggestion. Bill took over as their ringleader.

"Yes!" he declared belligerently. "We're not going unless Mr Purvis comes too."

Mary put up her hands to soothe her rioting brood.

"All right," she said. "I'm quite sure that Gerald will be only too delighted for Mr Purvis to come to the party as well."

Downstairs, Gerald was just giving Nesta instructions to buy food for the party, when Mary came into his office. She looked over at Gerald and asked, "Am I intruding?"

Gerald was exuding confidence and bonhomie as he crossed over to welcome her.

"Good gracious, no! Come in!" He glanced over at Nesta, who was hovering in the doorway, and smiled

pointedly. "Nesta, do close the door, will you!" As Nesta
went out and closed the door behind her, he turned back
to Mary and asked. "As a matter of fact, I was just about
to come back upstairs to see you . . ." He cleared his
throat before going on diplomatically. "It's about that
little favour I was going to ask of you . . ."

"It's funny you should say that . . ." Mary cut in on
him, ". . . because that's why I came down here. To ask
a little favour of you."

Gerald had not heard her. Pacing the room, he was still
preoccupied with his own thoughts, as he tried to find the
right words to phrase his request.

"Yes, it concerns my father," he said at last. "You see
he's getting on a bit . . ."

Mary was equally preoccupied with her thoughts as
she struggled to frame her petition.

"I feel a bit embarrassed asking you," she stammered,
"but John had arranged to take the children to the cinema
again tonight . . ."

Gerald was still not listening, and continued to go on
about his father.

"It's not just his age . . ." he laboured to make his
words sound plausible, ". . . but, how shall I put it, well,
senility affects people in different ways. In my father's
case, he has this strange delusion that . . ." He suddenly
looked across at Mary as his enemy's name came to him
through the ether. "John?" he frowned.

"John Purvis!" Mary smiled. "As I was saying, he had
arranged, apparently, to take the kids to the cinema . . ."

Gerald was clearly agitated.

"But you're having supper with me!" he protested.

"Of course we are," Mary smiled reassuringly. "We're
all looking forward to it. It's just that it leaves John at a
bit of a loose end, so I knew you wouldn't mind if he came
along to supper tonight as well." She smiled her appreciation of his kindness and understanding and turned to
make for the door. "Must dash! See you later," she
called, blowing him a friendly kiss and darting out through
the door.

Gerald stared after her in blank disbelief. Everything had been going perfectly according to plan, and now bloody John Purvis had to push his smooth, ingratiating nose in. He slumped wearily into his chair and, in the blackest of black depressions, reached out for the telephone and slowly began to dial.

"Hello father," he began bravely. "Slight change of plan." He winced in anticipation of the inevitable explosion in his ear.

"But we settled everything yesterday!" his father roared.

"Right!" Gerald gulped. "Amazing how little problems crop up just when you least expect them."

Bitterly disappointed by this cancellation, old Henry was in a thoroughly bad temper.

"Well," he growled. "What the hell is it?"

Gerald groped for a plausible excuse as he struggled for survival.

"Yes . . . !" he exclaimed, having to play it completely by ear. ". . . It's young Toby's sports day today. Foolish of me to have forgotten it. Thank Heavens Mary just reminded me . . . Well! There you are . . . Can't let the little fellow down. Trouble is, we won't be back until late."

"How late?" The old man demanded.

"Oh, very late, I'm afraid," Gerald replied, taking a handkerchief and mopping his brow. "It's all the way over to Winchfield. About a forty-mile round trip. Of course," he added cunningly," 'we could still meet, if you felt like traipsing over there."

"Certainly not!"

"That's what I hoped . . . er thought!" he hastily corrected himself. "Right, well, call you tomorrow, father. We'll arrange something, don't worry. Bye for now!" Without giving his father the chance of taking the last word, he slammed the receiver down.

Nesta had done them proud. With the help of the children, she had moved the dining-room table into the conservatory, and it was soon groaning under the weight of jellies, blancmanges, trifles, cakes and sandwiches, sausages on sticks and gallons of soft drinks.

Once the party got under way, the children swarmed round the table like bees round a honey pot and within a few minutes the more than ample supplies of goodies had become sadly depleted, and the expressions on the children's faces as they tucked into their second and third helpings was a fair indication that her choice of menu had been a popular one.

Gerald managed to disguise his loathing for Purvis and they both mingled with Mary, Adela and the children, helping themselves at the buffet table and chatting together as they nibbled at the confections in their hands. Suddenly Purvis, who was in ebullient form, leaped up onto a chair and began to lead the others in singing,

Happy birthday to you,
Happy birthday to you,

By the third line of the song, Mary and all the children were giving it full voice and even Adela was making a sizeable contribution to the volume, although struggling a little with the words.

Happy birthday dear Gerald,
Happy birthday to you.

In the midst of the applause that followed, Purvis could be heard above the others calling, "Speech! Speech!"

The cry was immediately taken up by the others and the boys joined with Purvis in propelling a reluctant and acutely embarrassed Gerald to the centre of the room. Faced with no alternative, he put up his hands for silence and stammered uncomfortably, "Really no . . . Just to say thank you for coming and . . . er . . . yes, well . . ." He was looking for a way out of making a speech when he spotted David's empty plate and turned to him. "David, your plate's empty. Can't have that!" he laughed weakly, moving away from the centre of the floor.

At that moment, Nesta came hurrying out of the kitchen and moved across the room to them.

"I'll be off now then, Mr Parish," she announced.

"Everything's out on the table, so you won't need me now."

"Well, thank you for all your hard work, Nesta, but won't you stay and have something to . . ."

"No thank you, Mr Parish," she replied as she went to the door. "I really have to go. I'm meeting a friend, and we're going to see a film."

As Nesta made her way across the hall to the front door of the house, she came face to face with Harold Searl, who had just stepped inside. He addressed her in a hoarse whisper.

"Is his nibbs in?"

She stopped dead in her tracks, fastening her gaze on the unsavoury-looking little man in front of her.

"We thought you were in Manchester!" she gasped in astonishment.

"I was," he leered, glancing furtively around the hall before fixing her with his more stable eye and whispering, "Look, I'd better speak to him."

She pursed her lips and eyed him disdainfully.

"I'm not sure if he's in," she lied.

Harold pushed past her and nodded towards the office.

"I'll be in there," he grinned cockily.

Nesta heaved a great sigh of disapproval, swept past him to the office door, took a key from her handbag and let him into the office.

"I'll go and check," she said, turning on her heel and stomping down the hall to the flat.

Nesta turned back to the party, which was in full swing.

"Excuse me, Mr Parish, there's someone to see you." she announced.

Gerald glanced at his watch and frowned.

"At this time?"

She gave him a knowing look and laid great stress on her words, as she confided:

"I think it's rather urgent!"

He hesitated for a moment, then turned to Purvis and Mary.

"Excuse me!" he muttered, moving away from them

and following Nesta out of the room.

Harold was pacing restlessly up and down in Gerald's office, glancing up casually at the portrait of the old Judge on the wall. He reacted as he heard the sound of footsteps in the hall and Gerald's voice just outside the door.

"Thank you, Nesta. Good night!"

As Nesta's footsteps disappeared down the hall, the door opened and Gerald entered and went straight through to his own office. He looked hopefully at the private eye.

"You've got something for me? You've found some dirt on Purvis?"

Harold shook his head dolefully.

"I'm thinking of your money, Gerald. That's why I came back now. To save another night's expenses." He shrugged and continued to shake his head. "I'm wasting my time," he lamented. "Purvis is as pure as the driven snow."

Gerald couldn't hide his bitter disappointment at the failure of Harold's expedition, and sank dejectedly into his chair.

"Surely there must be . . ."

"You sent me on a wild goose chase," Harold protested. "Go and find some dirt, you said. What dirt?" he snorted in disgust. "It's like saying, 'Go and prove the pandas at the zoo are really Chinese spies!'"

Gerald looked up at him sadly, an utterly defeated man.

"All right, Harold," he smiled wanly. "Send me your bill."

"Sorry Gerald," Harold stammered, uncomfortably. "I checked everything . . . every aspect of this Purvis fellow. He's a pillar of society."

Gerald had heard enough, and put up his hand in a gesture of acceptance.

"Right!" he said dejectedly. "That's enough."

"I mean," Harold went on regardless, "even his wife is Chairman of the local Parent, Teachers Association . . ."

Sick of the whole sorry business, Gerald cut right across him.

"You did your best, Harold. Thank you." Suddenly something Harold had said half-registered in his troubled mind.

"His what?" he asked, staring blankly at Harold.

Harold stared back at him, equally bewildered.

"His wife," he replied, flatly.

The blood was flowing back into Gerald's veins.

"Why the hell didn't you tell me he was married?" he exclaimed excitedly.

Harold was all at sea, totally bemused by Gerald's change of attitude.

"For the same reason I didn't tell you he's got three kids," he replied. "You told me you wanted dirt, remember? I hardly considered . . ."

Gerald jumped up excitedly from his desk.

"Purvis is married with three kids!" he exclaimed.

"Right." Harold nodded. "And his wife is Chairman of the Parent, Teachers Association. What's wrong with that?"

Gerald tried to hold his feeling of jubilation in check as he composed himself and turned to Harold.

"Nothing, Harold." He smiled. "Just order yourself a bottle of champagne with dinner tonight and put it on my bill." He turned on his heel and swept briskly out of the office, leaving a very confused private eye staring after him.

Chapter Seventeen

A Nasty Departure

Mary looked anxiously at her watch. Gerald had been gone some time and she began to wonder whether some emergency or other had taken him away from the house, preventing him from returning to his 'birthday party'. The children were still enjoying themselves, but it was getting near their bedtime, and though, during the school holidays, she allowed them to stay up later, there was a compelling reason why she wanted them in bed early that night. The reason was standing at her side in the shape of John Purvis, the life and soul of the party, jollying things along and livening up the party as he beamed benevolently at the dancing children. In odd glances at Mary, however, he allowed the mask to slip sufficiently to reveal his intense irritation that they were still lumbered with the children. He had his own plans for the evening, and they didn't include the children. It seemed such bad form to break up Gerald's party and she'd been hoping he'd return before they had to take their leave of him, but as the irritable looks from Purvis increased in frequency, she became increasingly aware of his growing impatience. Finally, and with some reluctance, she called a halt to the festivities.

"All right, children!" she called. "Bedtime!"

As the chorus of groans went up from the children, the door opened and Gerald strode briskly into the room, crossing straight over to join Mary. She smilingly acknowledged him as she renewed her call to the children.

"Come on now, children! Say thank you and goodnight to Mr Parish!"

Adela moved in quickly to usher them into line, and

they mumbled their disgruntled goodnights as they filed past Gerald, Mary turned to Gerald, and prepared to take their leave.

"Well!" she smiled. "We must be going too. Thank you, it was lovely . . ."

"Nonsense!" Gerald exclaimed, taking full command of the situation. "You and John must stay and have a birthday drink with me. I insist!" He smiled to himself as he saw Purvis glancing anxiously at Mary and, regardless of his enemy's obvious discomfiture, pressed on, looking directly at them and beaming expansively. "Now! What will it be?"

Mary glanced anxiously at Purvis and smiled nervously.

"Er . . . a gin and tonic would be fine," she replied.

"One gin and tonic coming up!" he cried, pouring generously from both bottles at once. Handing the glass to Mary, he turned to Purvis. "And you, John?"

"Scotch, thank you," Purvis replied, flatly.

"And two Scotches!" he beamed at Purvis as he took two glasses and poured from the whisky bottle. He took the drinks in his hands and turned away from the drinks table, hesitated, and looked across at Mary. "Tell me something, Mary! The children all go to school locally, don't they?"

It seemed a strange question to come from Gerald, and Mary eyed him curiously as she replied.

"Yes."

He smiled and nodded his head, as he continued across the room and handed a drink to Purvis, looking him directly in the eye.

"Out of interest, John," he smiled disarmingly, "are you a member of the P.T.A.?" He looked at him earnestly as he explained, "That's short for Parent, Teachers Association."

Purvis froze momentarily, and glanced anxiously at Mary.

She looked from Purvis to Gerald, and, thinking the question had been directed at her, replied, "No, I'm not a member, actually."

Purvis's startled reaction had not escaped Gerald's notice, and he was already savouring his moment of triumph. He was deliberately casual as he continued to stick the pins into his discomfited enemy.

"Just wondered. I always think it such a good idea. Parents and teachers getting together regularly. What do you think, John?"

"Yes. Well . . ." Purvis stumbled, ". . . can't see any harm in it."

"No," Gerald said earnestly. "Neither can I! In fact, I'd go so far as to say that Parent, Teacher Associations are pretty worthwhile organisations!"

"Yes," Purvis agreed and, anxiously trying to change the subject, commented, "Well, the party went down well with the kids."

Gerald appeared not to have heard him as he ploughed on relentlessly.

"I suppose they have Parent, Teacher Associations all over the country!" he turned smilingly to John. "Manchester for instance. I bet they have one or two there!"

The colour was perceptibly draining from Purvis's cheeks as he replied.

"Must do."

"Oh! But how silly of me," Gerald exclaimed, a little dramatically. "How could I expect you to know? You're not married, are you?"

Purvis looked distinctly uncomfortable as Gerald deliberately waited for his answer. His eyes flickered from Gerald to Mary as he snapped, "No. No, I'm not!"

"So you wouldn't have any children of your own." Gerald smiled, indulgently. "So how would you know about Parent, Teachers Associations?"

Mary finished her drink, put the glass down on the table and smiled across at Gerald.

"Well, that was lovely, Gerald. Thank you for the drink."

Gerald ignored her attempt to break up the party and continued to address himself to Purvis.

"Funny!" he mused. "Talking of Parent, Teacher Associations, I've just remembered, I know someone who's a chairman of one." He flickered his fingers, impatiently. "What's her name, now?"

Mary had been watching the proceedings and was slightly puzzled when she saw Purvis staring, seemingly transfixed, at Gerald. She shrugged and turned to go.

"Look, I must go now. Make sure the kids are all tucked up," she said as she crossed over to the door. "Thanks again, Gerald. See you later John!" She turned in the doorway when there was no response from Purvis, who was still staring at Gerald and didn't seem to have heard her. Raising her voice, she called again. "You are coming up for a nightcap, John?"

Purvis turned round sharply to face her.

"Er . . ." he began to stammer, acutely aware of Gerald's eyes looking right through him. "I er . . . I'd better not." He glanced nervously at his watch, studiously avoiding Mary's eyes when he looked up again. "I should really get the next train up north. Have to be at the factory crack of dawn tomorrow."

Mary was watching him curiously. It was the first she'd heard about him having to be at the factory in the morning and it certainly hadn't figured in the arrangements they'd made earlier together. She looked at him for a moment, took in a short quick breath and noticeably stiffened.

"Okay," she said quietly. "See you, then." She went out through the door and closed it behind her.

There was a long silence as Purvis slowly finished his drink. Then in a sudden outburst of feeling, he turned to Gerald and exclaimed, "How the hell did you find out?"

Gerald smiled maliciously. He had suffered agonies because of Purvis, and now that their positions had changed and the boot was on the other foot, he wasn't going to let up on his vanquished enemy. His star was suddenly in the ascendant and he meant to keep it there.

"It doesn't matter how I found out," he replied. "What does matter is that you go upstairs and have that nightcap with Mary."

Purvis frowned and then his brow unfurrowed as he began to hope Gerald was letting him off the hook. Hopes that were soon dashed as Gerald went on.

"And tell her that you're married with three children!"

Purvis put down his empty glass and moved over to the door.

"I've got a better idea," he said coolly. "I'll get that train." He was half-way through the door, when suddenly he turned and snapped venomously, "You tell her!"

Gerald watched him storm out into the hall and seconds later heard the front door slam behind him. He smiled quietly to himself, crossed over to the drinks table and replenished his glass. For a few moments he stood lost in contemplation, then he glanced up at the ceiling, raised his glass in a silent toast, and slowly sipped its contents.

It was a rather subdued Mary that came down the stairs into the living-room, having tucked up the children for the night. She was bothered by the strange behaviour of John Purvis, and couldn't understand why he had suddenly changed his mind and hared off on the first train he could catch. If he had to be back at the factory next morning, why hadn't he mentioned it before? She had known him for some months and he'd never behaved like that before — it seemed completely out of character. She was racking her brains to think of a possible reason for his erratic behaviour when she heard a tap on the front door, and, thinking it might be John Purvis, rushed over to open it. As the door opened, she was astonished to see Gerald standing there, holding a plate of jelly in each hand.

"Ah . . . these were left over," he smiled, nervously. "I thought you might have more use for them than I."

Still a little bewildered by Gerald's sudden appearance, she took the jellies from him and half turned to go back into the flat.

"Thank you Gerald." As she looked back, waiting to push the door to, he was still hovering in the doorway, looking strangely uncomfortable.

"Yes . . . er," he stammered uncertainly, pointing alternately to the jellies in each hand, ". . .er, I think that one's the raspberry and er . . . that one's the strawberry." He moved closer to peer at them. "Difficult to tell in this light."

"I don't suppose they'll notice the difference," she smiled. Gerald showed no inclination to go as she stood there, the jellies shivering in her hands, waiting for him to move so that she could close the door. "Well . . ." she said, turning again to go inside.

"Well . . ." he interrupted her and took a step towards her. ". . . er, the thing is, there's something I have to say to you. To tell you, really. It's a matter of some delicacy."

She stood back to let him enter.

"You'd better come in, then," she said.

She deposited the jellies on the table and turned back to join him, watching him curiously as she waited to hear what delicate matter he wanted to discuss. He didn't find it easy to know where to begin.

"It's about John Purvis."

She started involuntarily, and her reply had a guarded edge.

"Yes?" She looked up defiantly and saw Gerald looking directly into her eyes. He wore a preoccupied look as though he was having some difficulty in framing the words he had to utter. It was some moments before he spoke.

"He's, er . . ." he sighed and tried again. "He's . . . I don't think he's quite the right person for you."

Mary's face darkened as she bristled angrily.

"I think I'm the better judge of that."

"What I really mean is . . ." Gerald persisted," he's not really free."

"Free?" Mary echoed, staring blankly at him.

Gerald was finding it heavy going, and Mary wasn't being particularly helpful. He paused to get his breath before going on to say, "Yes. He's not available."

She rounded on him sharply.

"Available for what?" she demanded.

He looked at her appealingly, imploring her to understand what he was trying to say.

"Available for . . . What I'm trying to say is that he's already tied up."

"Tied . . . !" she moved right up to him and looked him squarely in the eye. "Look Gerald!" she said. "If you've got something to say, why don't you just say it?"

If there was one thing he'd always admired about Mary, it was her directness, and she'd made her point: he had been going round in circles and getting nowhere. As he looked back into her eyes, the suggestion of a half-apologetic smile flickered momentarily across his lips. He took a deep breath, and spoke quietly as he told her.

"John Purvis is married. With three children."

She stared back at him in shattered silence and it was some moments before she spoke.

"He can't be!" Her words were barely audible, and in her gaze was the pained, uncomprehending look of a wounded animal.

All the feelings of triumph Gerald had experienced when he sent John Purvis on his way evaporated in the overwhelming sea of compassion welling up inside him. Compassion tinged with guilt at the dubious motives that impelled him to break up the relationship. He felt no remorse about the outcome — she'd have been bound to find out about Purvis sooner or later and, that being the case, the sooner the better. It was just that he hated to see her suffering, and in a strange way he could feel her pain as he looked back at the haunted eyes that were apealing to him, begging him to say it wasn't true. There was genuine sorrow in his voice and he spoke gently as he confirmed her worst fears.

"I'm afraid he is."

She stood, motionless, for a moment; then turned away and sank, slowly, into a chair. Realising that he could do nothing for her very private grief, Gerald silently turned and went downstairs, shutting the door behind him.

Chapter Eighteen

A Strange Delusion

Nesta's arms were full of loose papers when the telephone rang. The filing cabinet was already overstuffed with bulging files, and she was facing up to the somewhat daunting task of making room for the huge bundle in her arms. She made a desperate attempt to get rid of the papers by stuffing them into the drawer, but to no avail, and she was still clutching the ungainly bundle as she staggered over to the telephone and with great difficulty lifted the receiver to her ear.

"Gerald Parish's office," she called, her voice distorted by the contortions of her body as she struggled to hold onto the papers. A voice barked in her ear, "Put him on!"

"Oh!" she gasped. "That's his father, isn't it?"

"You know damned well it is!" old Henry snorted back. "Put Gerald on the line!"

"I'm afraid he's out at the moment, sir," she replied with difficulty as the papers began to slip. "Can I get him to call you back?"

"No!" the voice thundered. "Just give him a message." Nesta looked wildly around her as she falteringly replied, "Just a moment, sir . . ." In her position, taking a message was easier said than done. She struggled to get the bundle of papers under one arm, transferred the telephone to the same hand and reached for the pad and ballpoint with the other. With the biro finally poised in her hand over the pad she was ready to take the message. "Right!" she exclaimed into the mouthpiece.

The old Judge, furious at having been kept waiting, began to dictate at an impossible speed.

"I've had enough, do you hear?" he roared. "I'm sick

to death of puerile excuses, one after another. I will not be fobbed off a moment longer . . .''

Nesta was writing furiously, trying to keep up with the breakneck pace Henry was setting. There was nothing she could do about the sheaf of papers under her arm, which were gradually detatching themselves and floating down onto the floor.

''I came over to this country to see my grandchildren, and see them I will. I'll be there for lunch and Gerald needn't bother to call me and try to wriggle out of it, because I'm not accepting any calls. Got that?''

Despite her frantic efforts to keep up, Nesta was way behind and was still scratching away on the pad.

''To see my grandchildren . . .'' she muttered as she continued to write. The ballpoint almost fell from her hand as old Henry exploded.

''For God's sake, you can remember a simple message, can't you?''

Drained of energy by her exertions, her cramped hand fell limply onto the pad as she panted, ''Yes sir, I was just . . .''

''Good! Then just give it to him!''

As the phone slammed down at the other end, she gazed at the jumble of notes on the pad in front of her, put down her ballpoint and slowly replaced the receiver onto its rest. Her eyes turned forlornly to the papers scattered on the floor all around her. Heaving a huge sigh, she creaked down on her knees and began the laborious task of picking them up and sorting them into some sort of order. She was still crawling about on her hands and knees when, some minutes later, Gerald arrived at the office. As he gazed at her in astonishment, she looked up wearily to say:

''Your father phoned, just this second, Mr Parish.''

He smiled down at her benevolently, as he stepped past her and crossed to the door.

''Told him I was out and I'd call him back. Hm?''

She swivelled round on her knees and looked up at him.

''Yes sir, but . . .''

''Good!'' he beamed, as he disappeared through the

door. Nesta scrambled painfully to her feet, steadied herself for a moment by holding onto the desk and, when the giddiness went from her head, followed him into his office.

Unaware of her presence, Gerald was sitting behind his desk, dictating into the Dictaphone.

"When you've sorted out your immaculate filing system, Nesta," he smiled to himself at the humorous touch he had put on tape, "a letter to Johnson, Row and Noughton. Dear Sir . . ." He suddenly noticed Nesta hovering at the other side of the desk.

"Well?" he exclaimed, smiling up at her.

"I'm afraid you won't be able to phone your father back."

Gerald's eyes lit up hopefully.

"He's left the country? He's gone home?"

"No, Mr Parish. He said . . ." a puzzled look came into her eyes as she continued. "I didn't quite understand, but he said something about seeing his grandchildren."

Gerald stiffened, and there was a look of alarm in his eyes as he demanded, "When?"

Nesta eyed him uncertainly and gave a little nervous cough before coming to the gist of old Henry's message.

"Today. He said he's coming round for dinner, and there's no point in your ringing him back and trying to wriggle out of it because he's not accepting any calls."

"My God!" Gerald gasped.

"He seemed under the impression . . ." she looked at him across the desk curiously, ". . . that his grandchildren were living here."

"Ah! Yes . . . well!" Gerald blustered, getting up from his chair. "Don't worry about it, Nesta." He crossed over to the door and turned to explain. "He's old, you see. He has these delusions . . . yes . . . er . . . well," he laughed, hollowly. "See you later."

She followed him anxiously through to the outer office, and was just in time to see him disappearing through the entrance door to the hall. Utterly bemused, she stood staring after him for a few moments, then sighed and,

129

holding onto a chair for support, slowly lowered herself onto her knees, to finish the task of picking up and sorting the papers on the floor.

Gerald had just reached the foot of the stairs when the front door opened and David and Bill stepped into the hall, carrying a model aeroplane they'd been flying. He turned from the stairs and moved towards them.

"Do you know if your mother's in?" he asked.

Bill glanced at his watch and shook his head.

"No chance! Another couple of hours at least."

David turned to explain.

"She's at the hairdresser's."

"I see," Gerald replied, thinking feverishly. "Well, if you see her before I do, I want you to tell her something for me."

The two boys exchanged glances before Bill replied, without enthusiasm, "Okay."

"Yes," Gerald went on to explain. "I am going to cook you all a very special dinner this evening. Only, as my flat's a bit small and there's rather a lot of you, I know she won't mind if I use your kitchen and we eat it . . ." he nodded his head, indicating the flat above, "up there!"

David began to look interested.

"What are we going to have?" he asked.

"Crown Roast of Lamb, cooked with herbs, spices and honey!"

Gerald's description of the treat in store for them brought a grimace to Bill's face.

"Sounds revolting," he commented.

"I can assure you it's quite delicious," Gerald retorted, a little hurt by the suggestion that any of his gourmet creations could be anything else.

David looked at him curiously.

"Why a special dinner tonight?" he asked.

"Ah well!" Gerald replied, mysteriously. "There is a particular reason, which you will all know about in due course; but I think I'd better speak to your mother about it first."

Bill shrugged his shoulders and glanced at David.

"Okay. See you," he said to Gerald as they passed him, carrying their model aircraft up the stairs.

He watched them until they passed out of sight on the landing, then stood for a moment in the hall getting his thoughts in order.

"Ingredients!" he mused aloud. "Yes, I must get some basil and . . . clover honey. Right!" He turned and strode briskly down the hall and straight into the outer office.

Nesta had succeeded in gathering up all the papers from the floor and was back at the filing cabinet trying to find the right files for them to go into.

"'C' . . . 'C' . . . 'C' for Conveyancing," she muttered to herself, holding the huge bundle in one hand as she fingered through the files in the cabinet with the other. She was totally engrossed in the job she was doing and quite unprepared for the shock when the door burst open and Gerald charged into the room. Startled almost out of her wits, her reaction was so violent that the papers shot from her hand and scattered themselves all over the floor once again.

Gerald stopped dead in his tracks and stared in horror at the scores of important documents lying all around his feet. He was about to comment, when he suddenly remembered that he was in a hurry, turned to a very distraught Nesta, and said, "Just going shopping, Nesta. I won't be long." He looked from her to the papers on the floor and commented, pointedly, "I can see you have plenty to occupy you while I'm out."

She was almost in tears as he went out through the door. It just wasn't her day. As his footsteps died away in the hall, she turned back to contemplate the daunting task in front of her. She sniffed, braced herself, and carefully levered herself down onto the floor to do the job all over again.

"Good morning."

She looked up, startled, then breathed again as she saw an elderly gentleman standing in the open doorway.

"Sorry . . . I . . . er . . ." she stammered apologetically, indicating the chaotic mess of papers on the floor, ". . . had a slight accident."

The old man displayed not the slightest concern for her problem as he demanded, "Where is he?"

Nesta stared up at the stranger blankly.

"Mr Parish?" she asked.

"Yes?" He inclined his ear towards her, waiting for her to continue.

Completely thrown by his reaction, she looked at him questioningly.

"Yes?" she repeated.

The old man snorted impatiently, pulled himself together and after a deep breath began to enunciate with shattering clarity, "Yes . . . I'm . . . Mr . . . Parish! Where's my son?"

As the realisation dawned on her, Nesta struggled to her feet and looked him directly in the eye.

"Ah . . . yes of course!" she exclaimed, crossing over to the communicating door and indicating the portrait on the wall. "I didn't recognise you without your wig and gown and things."

The old Judge pushed his way past her in Gerald's office and stopped opposite his portrait. Nesta watched from the doorway; her hands clasped together and her face set into a peculiar, subservient smile, as Henry grunted up at his likeness on the wall.

"Huh! Surprised he hasn't burnt it by now." He looked across at Nesta, remarking, "I wouldn't have kept his for fifteen minutes, let alone fifteen years." As he turned and went back past Nesta into the outer office, her smile had given place to an expression of tight-lipped indignation. "Not that anyone would want to paint a total failure like Gerald," he grunted.

Nesta bristled inside that the old Judge could speak in such a derogatory manner about his own son, and her feelings of hostility were reflected in her voice, which took on a tone of frigid politeness.

"He shouldn't be gone long, sir. He's gone out shopping."

Henry turned to glower at her as he growled contemptuously.

"Huh! Typical. Shopping! Woman's work!"

She followed him anxiously as he prowled out into the hall, and was alarmed when he stopped to glare at the greenery festooning the staircase. Remembering what Gerald had told her about his father's strange delusions, she stepped in quickly to prevent what could be an embarrassing situation for the people upstairs.

"Joanna's," she explained, indicating the greenery. "One of the children's upstairs."

Henry turned to grunt at her.

"Huh! Upstairs, are they?"

Her heart missed a beat as the old man started to manoeuvre his way up through the greenery. She had to stop him at all costs, and raised her voice as she scurried up behind him on the stairs.

"Urrgh!" The strange noise at his elbow brought Henry round sharply to stare at her as she continued, "If you'd like to wait in Mr Parish's office?"

"You wait in his office!" he thundered, as he continued to climb the stairs. "I'm going to see my grandchildren!"

Nesta was getting rapidly out of her depth, and quite unable to cope with the situation. The delusions Gerald had spoken of were, obviously, far worse than she'd imagined.

"I don't think you'll find them up there," she cried despairingly. Her hopes rose a little when he stopped suddenly in his tracks, but faded immediately as he turned to glare belligerently down at her.

"Joanna, Bill, Toby, Richard and David!" he barked. "Are you telling me that they don't live here?"

She stared back at him in blank amazement and her voice was barely audible as she squeaked, "Oh yes . . . they live here." As the old man snorted and turned away from her, she cried out wildly, "But you're making a mistake! They're not yours!"

The Judge stopped, turned round slowly to face her and, fixing her with the eye that once struck terror into the hearts of hardened criminals, pronounced his reasoned judgement.

"You are either mad or just plain stupid!" he decreed. "I can only put it down to the fact that you work for that equally idiotic son of mine." With a final explosive grunt, he turned and continued to ascend the stairs, making slow and laborious progress up through the plant life, and leaving an utterly confused Nesta staring unbelievingly after him.

Chapter Nineteen

The Unexpected Guest

Toby was on his way upstairs to tidy his room (he had been warned that if he didn't, he would not be going to the cinema with the others next Wednesday), when a knock on the front door caused him to double back to answer it. As he swung the door open, an unfamiliar gruff voice greeted him.

"Ah! You must be Toby."

He stared up at the old man standing in the doorway.

"How did you know that?" he asked.

"From the photographs of course!" Henry exclaimed, striding past him into the room and turning round to face him. "Now then!" he said, peering right down into Toby's face. "Do you know who I am?"

Toby glanced up at him as he closed the front door.

"Haven't the faintest idea," he replied. "Have you come to see Mummy?"

The old Judge bristled slightly that the boy could be so dense — he must have known for weeks that he was coming to see them. "I've come to see all of you!" he said, with as much patience as he could muster. "I'm Henry Parish."

Toby looked up, interested.

"Any relation to Gerald Parish?" he asked innocently.

"Of course I am!" Henry exploded, irritably. "I'm his father!"

"Oh . . ." Toby smiled, happy to have established the stranger's identity. "Well, if you'll excuse me, I've got to go and tidy up my room."

Old Henry was bursting with indignation, and as Toby turned to cross over to the stairs, moved rapidly past him and barred his progress.

"Just a minute!" he commanded. "Now look, I didn't expect a brass-band welcome, but I do expect a little civility."

Toby couldn't think what he'd done to offend the old man, and there was a confused look in his eyes as he echoed, "Civility?"

"Well, you could ask me if I'd like to sit down," the Judge glared fiercely. "Perhaps offer me a drink."

Toby shrugged indifferently. If that was all the old man wanted, he was happy to oblige.

"Okay. Sit down!" Henry winced at the boy's total lack of social graces but nevertheless responded to his offhanded invitation, sitting down on the sofa and watching as Toby crossed over to the kitchen, turning at the door to ask, "Orange squash do?"

"No it will not do!"

Somewhat taken aback by the old man's rejection of his offer, Toby racked his brains for an acceptable alternative.

"Lemon squash?" he suggested tentatively.

Henry snorted in disgust, raised himself from the low, squelchy sofa and eyed Toby severely.

"I can see that you have inherited Gerald's total lack of etiquette. Even at your tender age, you should know that you offer someone of my advanced age a glass of dry sherry before luncheon."

Toby shrugged again and crossed over to the drinks table.

"Okay. Sherry it is," he sighed.

Henry gave a resigned grunt and peered around at the furnishings as Toby took the nearest glass to hand, a half-pint pot, filled it to the brim with sherry, and, taking great care not to spill the contents, carried it over and offered it to him.

"My God!" Henry exclaimed, staring at the tankard in the boy's hand. "Is that how my son drinks it?"

Toby shook his head, smiling disarmingly.

"He drinks Scotch!" He was a little perplexed when the Judge made no movement to take the drink from him and, after a moment's pause, looked up at him and asked, "Do you want this or don't you?"

"Certainly not!" Henry snorted indignantly. "Pour it back into the bottle at once!"

Toby sighed and looked down at the brimming half-pint pot in his hand, wondering how he could get its contents back through the narrow neck of the sherry bottle. The old man didn't seem to know what he wanted: he'd tried to please him and a fat lot of good it had done him — all he'd got in return was a load of brickbats. Resignedly, he turned and headed back to the drinks table to begin the tedious task of pouring the sherry back into the bottle.

Just then, Richard came running down the stairs into the living-room, stopping as he saw the old man looking round at him.

"Hello!" he said, brightly.

"Now let me see . . ." Henry pondered, eyeing him up and down. "You must be . . . Richard, isn't it?"

"Yes," Richard replied, surprised that the stranger should know his name. He looked round at Toby, who wasn't having a great deal of success in getting the sherry back into the bottle and was spilling most of it onto the table. Glancing up and catching Richard's eye, Toby informed him, without noticeable enthusiasm, "He's Gerald's dad."

Richard turned round to face Henry and extended his hand.

"Pleased to meet you!" he smiled.

The old Judge took his hand and shook it firmly.

"That's better," he grunted, adding a little grudgingly, "Slightly more civilised than your brother."

"Toby!"

A raucous yell from the landing brought Henry round sharply, to see Joanna darting down the stairs and making a bee-line for Toby at the drinks table. Her intention was to yank him upstairs, by the ears if necessary, to tidy his bedroom as he'd promised her he would do. She stopped suddenly, horrified at the sight of the highly polished surface of the table swimming with sherry.

"Look at that mess you're making!" she gasped. "Mummy'll murder you if she sees that!"

The old Judge moved over and attempted to placate her and at the same time make the acquaintance of his 'granddaughter'.

"Ah . . . I'm afraid this is partly my fault," he began as she glared up at him. "I suggested that . . ."

That was as far as he got before Joanna rounded on him waspishly.

"Then you should be ashamed of yourself, encouraging him to do a stupid think like that! Who are you, anyway?" she demanded.

"Gerald's dad," Richard said.

"Huh!" she snorted, tossing her head in the air and moving to the kitchen. She stopped at the kitchen door, turned to face the Judge and said offhandedly, "Well, if you're waiting for Mummy, she should be back soon."

Bill and David had come down the stairs, unnoticed by the others, and had been standing at the foot of the stairs watching their firebrand of a sister as she ranted on at the old Judge. As she turned and went into the kitchen, Bill moved over to face Henry.

"So you're Gerald's dad?" Bill asked, looking at him with an expression of indolent curiosity.

Henry was incensed by the children's abrasive indifference, and the persistent way they referred to him in the common vernacular was too much to bear.

"Will you stop calling me that!" he exploded angrily. There was an uncomfortable silence as the boys exchanged confused glances with each other. Joanna came in briskly from the kitchen and crossed over to clean up the mess on the drinks table, stopping suddenly as she became aware of the silence all around her. She looked questioningly at each of her brothers in turn, but none of them spoke. Finally the silence was broken by Bill, who turned to the old Judge, who was still quivering from his outburst, and conceded generously, "Fine. We won't call you Grandad."

Somewhat placated by Bill's assurance, the old man began to grunt conciliatory noises, and this heartened

Toby to suggest helpfully, "Shall we call you Henry?"

"Certainly not!" he roared angrily. "You will show some respect and address me as 'Sir'!"

The Judge's thunder brought something of a forbidding, courtroom atmosphere to the Lamperts' living-room and for once all the children were completely subdued. As he continued to glare at them, they cast sidelong glances at each other, shuffling their feet in the uneasy, suffocating silence. They were all relieved when the front door opened and Adela entered, struggling under the weight of a load of shopping in her arms. As the eagle eyes switched to rivet themselves on her, the children felt a sense of release.

"Don't recognise you!" he said accusingly, before turning to the children and demanding, "Who is this young lady?"

"Adela. The au pair." Bill replied, going on to explain, "Her English isn't very good."

"Neither are your manners!" Henry snapped. "Take that shopping from her at once!"

There was no disobeying the Judge's command, and both Bill and Richard stepped forward smartly to relieve Adela of her burden.

Henry turned to face her, and the children watched in utter amazement as he inclined his head forward and twisted his features into a smile that indicated his extreme tolerance for foreigners. A little startled by the strange face smiling right at her, Adela cast furtive, appealing looks at the children, who were all faintly amused by her predicament. She looked back at him as he began to speak, enunciating each word clearly and distinctly for her benefit.

"How-do-you-do?" he leered benevolently.

She looked at him curiously.

"How do I do what?" she asked.

"No," Henry smiled, patiently. "You-mis-under-stand. The statement that I made was a 'greeting'. I'm enquiring as to your well-being. For instance, your state of health."

The smile never left his face as he watched her fumbling

in her pocket for her dictionary, and he nodded encouragement as she thumbed frantically through its pages.

"State?" she exclaimed, frowning and looking back to the dictionary to make sure she hadn't misread the entry. ". . . State?"

"State-of-health," he repeated helpfully.

She looked back to the dictionary and shook her head vigorously.

"No!" she explained. "State of Poland. Is my country."

The smile on the Judge's face, which he'd so patiently maintained throughout the exchange with Adela, began to uncrease as he realised he was getting nowhere.

"No, I . . ." he began to stammer as he struggled to find the words that would convey meaning to the blank, uncomprehending eyes staring up at him. Finally, in sheer frustration, he gave up the struggle. "It doesn't matter," he said, turning away and leaving a still confused Adela searching her little book for the meaning of his last remark.

At that moment, the front door opened and Mary returned from the hairdresser's, with the new 'hair do' very much in evidence.

Henry turned smilingly to greet her.

"Ah! Mary! Very pleased to meet you. Henry Parish!" he boomed, extending his hand to her.

Somewhat taken aback at the sight of a stranger in her living-room, she shook hands, a little uncertainly.

"Oh, er . . . Any relation to Gerald Parish?" she asked.

The old Judge suddenly fumed in exasperation.

"That's the second time I've been asked that! I'm his father, dammit!"

Mary was still confused and a little put out by the old man's display of temper. She had a hundred and one things on her mind, and could have done without such an unwarranted intrusion into the privacy of her home, but since he was Gerald's father, she put herself out to be civil to him.

"Oh. Well. I'm very pleased to meet you," she smiled coolly, and after a moment's hesitation said, "Excuse me a moment," and turned to Joanna, asking, "Joanna!

Did you put on the lunch, like I asked?''

Joanna nodded in the affirmative.

''In the oven. Should be ready soon.''

''Good! All right children, lay the table!'' She looked back at the old man, who showed no sign of moving, and tried to give him a gentle hint. ''Er . . . is Gerald not in his office?'' she asked.

The hint was lost on Henry, who bristled back sharply, ''I was informed by his secretary that he had gone out shopping.''

Mary was at a complete loss to know what to do. The man clearly had no intention of going, and it must have been obvious to him that the family were about to have their midday meal. She was prepared to go a long way in the interests of 'good-neighbourliness' but she had almost reached the limit as she fought back the impulse to show the disagreeable old man to the door.

''Were you . . . yes . . .'' she stammered. ''Well . . . look, if you have nothing else to do at the moment . . er, perhaps you'd like to join us for lunch?''

''That was the idea!'' he snapped, and as Mary and the children stared in shocked disbelief, crossed over to the drinks table and glared across the room at her. ''Perhaps I may be permitted a small glass of sherry, instead of the bath tub I was offered earlier?''

''Of course,'' Mary gulped, bitterly regretting her moment of weakness in inviting the man to stay for lunch. He was impossibly ill-mannered and not at all as she'd have expected Gerald's father to be. As the other children got on with the business of laying the table, Bill sidled up to her and spoke quietly into her ear.

''I've got a message for you,'' he said. ''It's from Mr Parish.'' Mary was completely lost, and nodded enquringly in the direction of old Henry, who was pouring himself a sherry at the drinks table. Bill shook his head and went on to explain. ''No, Gerald! He's cooking us all dinner tonight. Up here! Apparently there's a special reason, but he wanted to talk to you about it first.''

''I can't wait!'' she muttered to herself, turning on her heel and going out of the room into the kitchen.

Chapter Twenty

A Narrow Shave

Gerald had completed his shopping and was happy that he had been able to acquire all the ingredients necessary for the exotic gourmet dish he'd planned for dinner that night. He had to make a good impression on his father, and there was no doubt of the choice of menu pleasing him. The old autocrat was a bit of a gourmet himself and knew good food when he tasted it; it was about the only thing Gerald and his father had in common. He'd thought up a plausible story to persuade Mary to play along with him and pass her family off to his father as his grandchildren. He hadn't spoken to her about it yet, but there was still plenty of time before the old man arrived for dinner. At last, things were going well for him.

He was loaded with his purchases as he opened the front door and stepped, humming happily to himself, into the hall and went straight through to his office.

"Any messages?" he asked as he popped his head round the door.

Nesta closed the drawer of the filing cabinet and smiled triumphantly as she crossed over to her desk and picked up the note pad.

"Mr Wilkinson called about the County Court Summons regarding his dog fouling the footpath," she read from the pad.

Gerald shrugged his shoulders and waved his free arm dismissively.

"Sort that one out later," he said.

"And your father's arrived."

Gerald was already half-way out through the door.

"Fine. Thank you Nesta." He pointed to the carrier bag

in his hand. "A few preparations to be made. Dinner tonight." He smiled as he went out into the hall.

Having completed the irksome task of filing away the papers, Nesta settled herself down to knit away the time remaining before lunch. Before she had time to knit the first stitch, however, there was an almighty crash in the hall and seconds later Gerald's ashen face appeared round the door. As she looked up, he gasped unbelievingly, "My father's arrived?"

She nodded smilingly.

"You were right about him being eccentric," she exclaimed. "He went upstairs to the Lamperts' flat and . . ." she lowered her voice and leaned towards him, confidentially, ". . . and he thinks those kids are his grandchildren!"

Gerald was severely shocked by the news and spoke incoherently.

"He thinks . . . he does . . . my father . . ." He stared at Nesta, completely numbed by the shock.

Without comprehending his state of mind, Nesta continued to take him into her confidence.

"When I told him he was making a mistake, he told me I was mad!" she paused, wide-eyed and open-mouthed, to allow the ridiculousness of such a suggestion to sink in, before going on to modify the Judge's remarks about her. ". . . or being silly or something."

Gerald gazed at her, stupified by her crass stupidity.

"You told him . . . ! Nesta! How long have you been working for me?"

Nesta put her pen to her lips as she cast her eyes thoughtfully up to the ceiling.

"Let me see . . . Six . . . no, nearly seven years now." She smiled up at him.

He moved towards her and glared down at her, addressing her slowly and deliberately.

"In all those years, have you ever known me to defend a murder case?" he asked.

Nesta paused as the case histories of the past seven years churned through her mind. She called to mind several cases of poaching, many cases of 'drunk and disorderly', but not a single case of murder. She shook her head firmly as she replied, "No. Never, Mr Parish."

"There's always a first time, Nesta," he said menacingly. "Even if I'd be defending myself."

"Oh Mr Parish," she laughed. "Don't be silly! Who would you murd. . ." She suddenly stopped as the point of Gerald's threat came home to her.

"If ever you see my father again," Gerald warned, wagging his finger in her face, "you will keep your mouth shut! Do you understand? Whatever happens, you will keep your mouth tightly shut!" He pointed through the door to the food lying on the floor in the hallway. "Put that food in my flat!" he commanded.

Nesta was rushing around like a scalded cat in her anxiety to please.

"Yes Mr Parish," she said, wringing her hands nervously together. "And then will it be alright if I go?"

"Go?" Gerald blazed. "Go where?"

She pointed to the time on her watch.

"It's my dinner hour," she explained.

Gerald was speechless for a moment, and just stared at her as the realisation hit him. Then suddenly he exploded.

"Lunch hour, you idiot! That's why I'm in this mess, isn't it? He told you he was coming round for lunch, didn't he?"

As Nesta nodded her head miserably, he ranted on, "Lunch is at midday. Dinner is in the evening!"

There was a blank look in Nesta's eye.

"When's supper, then?" she squeaked.

"It doesn't matter!" Gerald stormed. "Lunch is lunch! And you've probably ruined my life! And if you have, you're fired!" He broke off and stood for a moment, panting for breath; then, as his breathing rate slowed down, he went on, a little more calmly. "In the meantime, type out a note for me!"

He paced up and down impatiently, as the befuddled Nesta searched aimlessly around for a piece of paper.

"Come on!" he growled.

144

Nesta redoubled her efforts and, in a state of complete panic, grabbed the nearest piece of paper she could find.

"Does it matter if it's on pink paper?" she trembled.

"I don't care if it's mauve with purple spots on it!" Gerald fumed. "Just put it in the damned typewriter!"

Nesta rushed to do his bidding and before her trembling fingers could get the paper level in the machine Gerald had already started to dictate.

"My father is quite mad. He has . . ."

Nesta looked up from the typewriter and interrupted, chattily, "Oh I wouldn't say he was mad, Mr Parish . . ." She broke off as she looked up at the murderous expression on Gerald's face.

"Just write it down!" he thundered.

"Oh, sorry," Nesta murmured, retreating into her shell and turning her attention to the typewriter.

"My father is . . . my father has deluded himself . . ." Gerald continued, ". . . deluded himself into believing that we are married . . ."

"Good gracious!" Nesta exclaimed, looking up wildly from the typewriter. "Why should he think you and I are married?"

Gerald clutched his head as he fought to retain his reason.

"He doesn't!" he cried desperately. "It's her upstairs, and will you just write the damned thing down?"

"Yes, Mr Parish."

Gerald glared at her for a few moments, sighed painfully and continued to dictate.

"That you and I are married . . . and that I am the father of your children. Please humour him. The truth could prove too much of a shock for the old fellow."

He watched over her shoulder as she typed, waited for her to finish, and then reached over and snatched the paper from the machine. A very startled Nesta looked up, just in time to see his back as he shot out through the door.

Upstairs, lunch was being served and the children were already sitting at the table. As Mary and the old Judge took their places at opposite ends of the table, Adela came

145

in from the kitchen and placed the enormous pie dish down on the table in front of Mary, who at once started to serve.

"I hope you like fish pie, Mr Parish?" she said, with all the civility she could muster.

"I can't say it's the top of my list, but I suppose it will suffice," Henry grunted, ungraciously. "Although I would have thought the occasion might have called for something slightly more adventurous." As Mary fumed inside at the old man's boorish ill manners, he went on to say, "But that's Gerald for you. Always was as tight as a drum. And while we're on the subject of Gerald, where is he? Why isn't he here?"

Mary glanced anxiously at the children, who were all equally confused by the Judge's question.

"Er, should he be?" she asked.

There was an astonished expression on Henry's face as he snorted.

"Of course he should! Doesn't he normally eat with you?"

"No, of course he doesn't," Mary replied.

"Why not?" Henry demanded.

Mary was completely flummoxed by the extraordinary cross-examination, and couldn't imagine what the old Judge was driving at.

"Well . . ." she replied, weakly. "He just doesn't. He never has."

The situation was far worse than old Henry had ever imagined. He'd never had a great deal of time for his son, but this sort of behaviour really was the limit.

"Never has!" he thundered. "Where in God's name does he eat, then?" He glared around the table as he waited for the answer to his question. It was Richard who at length found the temerity to break the heavy silence.

"Downstairs," he said, indicating the flat downstairs with a thumbs-down sign.

Henry was still rumbling with indignation at his son's outrageous behaviour, when the front door opened and the smiling prodigal entered the room.

146

"Hello father! . . . Everybody! . . . Sorry I'm a bit late . . ." Mary and the children watched in silence as Gerald casually collected a chair, carried it to the table and sat down. "Well!" he exclaimed, looking around the table. "You've obviously all got to know each other!" Through the corner of his eye, he could see his father's impassive expression and turned to face him for the first time in fifteen years. "Slight mix-up with my secretary." he smiled, glibly. "She thought . . . that is to say, she gave me the impression that you were coming to dinner."

Henry's reply was quite uncompromising.

"I distinctly said lunch," he snapped.

"Which she freely admits," Gerald beamed. "Her mistake, no doubt about that." He turned to Mary and lowered his voice as he said, "Bill may have mentioned to you about . . ."

"Dinner tonight!" Mary interrupted, relieved that things seemed to be sorting themselves out. "You were going to cook a special dinner for your father."

"Exactly!" He pulled the note Nesta had typed from his pocket and glanced at it anxiously as he went on to say, "I've done all the shopping, but I'm not sure about this bill, Mary." He passed the note across the table to her. "I think I may have been overcharged. What do you think?"

As Mary read the note in her hand, there was a growl from the other end of the table.

"Gerald!" Henry boomed, in a tone that demanded his son's attention. "I am somewhat disconcerted to learn that you never eat with your family."

"Slight exaggeration I think, father." Gerald laughed uncertainly, casting anxious glances at the children. "Occasionally, of course, I do have a snack down in my office. Right, Mary?"

Mary had read the note and rushed in to support Gerald's story.

"Yes, er . . . When I said he never eats with us, what I was actually saying was that it seems that way." She smiled up at Gerald as she added, "On account of the fact that's he's always so very busy."

Bill had not yet cottoned on to what was happening and started to argue.

"But he's never had a meal with us in his . . ."

He stopped abruptly as Mary thrust Gerald's note under his nose and said, hurriedly, "You're the mathematics genius in this house, Bill. Perhaps you'd like to check this?" As Bill took the note and began to read it, she turned to Henry and explained, "We like to involve the children in every aspect of . . ." As the words suddenly failed her, she turned to Toby and scolded him. "Toby! Your hands are filthy! How dare you sit down to the table with hands like that!"

"But I just washed them!" Toby protested, and would have said more if Mary hadn't trampled right on, smothering his outraged feelings.

"Not very well! Go and wash them again!" Without pausing for breath, she rounded on all the other children at the table. "In fact all of you, upstairs immediately and scrub your hands perfectly clean." As they began to murmur, discontentedly, she stood up and pointed to the stairs. "Go on! All of you! Right now!" she commanded. As the children rose, muttering under their breath, from the table, she turned to Bill and indicated the note in his hand. "You're in charge!" she said, giving him a meaningful look. "See that they all do — as — they — are — told." As the children went up the stairs, she gasped for breath and turned with a smile to Henry, who had been watching the proceedings in a state of utter bewilderment. "Sorry about that, Henry, but our motto is strict discipline where the children are concerned."

Gerald, who had watched Mary's performance with unadulterated admiration, chipped in, enthusiastically.

"Yes. Cleanliness is next to Godliness I always say and . . ."

His little platitude earned him a withering look from his father, who cut in on him gruffly, "I'm all for discipline of course, but . . . well, frankly, I didn't see that their hands were all that dirty."

"No," Gerald laughed uncertainly, "they have a knack of hiding them under the table." He pointed to his eye. "Where that lot's concerned, you have to have an experienced eye. Right, Mary?"

Mary laughed as she agreed.

"Right!"

Henry had been watching them curiously and there was a distinct note of disapproval in his voice as he commented curtly, "Apparently."

Gerald looked around uncomfortably and tried to switch the conversation to a less controversial topic.

"Well ... Let's not interfere with lunch!" he exclaimed, reaching forward and lifting the lid of the pie dish, and gazing at the contents. "Fish pie," he gulped, forcing his features into the semblance of a smile. "How nice."

"The children's favourite," Mary rushed to explain.

The smile was still fixed on Gerald's face as he gushed with forced enthusiasm:

"Quite!"

As Mary looked up, she could see Bill signalling to her from the stairs. She turned to Henry and excused herself before getting up from the table and crossing over to the foot of the stairs. Bill spoke quietly as he sought to clarify the children's brief.

"We just have to pretend that Gerald's our father. Is that it?" he asked.

Through the corner of her eye, Mary could see old Henry glaring curiously over in their direction, so she tried to keep her voice down.

"In a nutshell," she whispered. "Now go and tell the others and make sure they understand." Then, with her weather eye on Henry, she raised her voice for his benefit, shouting, "And make sure that they use that nailbrush!"

As Bill gave her a knowing wink and went back up the stairs, she turned and crossed back to her place at the table, smiling at Henry as she commented, "Little rascals!"

Henry dismissed her remark with a grunt and turned

his attention to the food on his plate.

"Well. No point in letting this get cold!" he said, taking up his fork and attacking his fish pie with considerable gusto. He took in a sizeable mouthful and, before he'd had time to register the pie's delicate flavour, had his fork already poised for a second mouthful. He chewed savagely for a couple of moments and then, suddenly, his jaw stopped moving and a peculiar glazed look came into his eyes. For some moments, his face was completely motionless, then he gulped and swallowed as the fork fell from his hand back onto the plate. He turned to Mary.

"Did I hear you say something about Gerald cooking a special dinner tonight?" he asked.

It was Gerald that answered, beaming from ear to ear.

"That's right, father."

The relief on the old Judge's face was unmistakable at having found a plausible excuse for not eating the rest of the pie on his plate.

"Ah!" he exclaimed, laying his knife beside the fork on his plate. "Better leave some room for that, don't you think?"

There was a sudden commotion as the children came tumbling down the stairs, dutifully showed their hands to their mother and rushed to take their places at the table. As they tucked into the fish pie, David looked over at Gerald and asked, "Could you pass the salt please, Daddy?"

When Gerald didn't respond, Bill nudged his elbow and grinned up at him.

"Daddy! David wanted the salt."

Lunch passed off reasonably peacefully after that, though the children played up with a slightly malicious glee to Gerald in his new role as their 'daddy'. Gerald was finding it all rather heavy going, and, after pouring a port for his father, Mary and himself, sought a diversion.

"Who's for a game of Monopoly," he said with a somewhat forced brightness, rubbing his hands together.

"Not if Toby's playing," Richard growled. "We'll be

here till midnight just explaining the rules to him.''

Mary was also feeling the strain, and cut in to suggest, ''I think that we should let your father decide what we do this afternoon. After all, he's our guest.''

As all eyes turned to the old Judge, he pondered thoughtfully before responding.

''Well . . . the only game I can remember playing as a child was 'charades',' he smiled.

Chapter Twenty-One

End of the Charade

There was a knock on the door and, as Mary opened it, Nesta entered the room and went straight over to Gerald.

"Sorry to interrupt, Mr Parish, but Mr Francis called," she said, a little breathlessly. "He asked if you would call him back."

"Yes, fine," Gerald smiled pleasantly. "I'll do that, Nesta. Thank you."

"He said tomorrow would do." She hesitated for a moment, hovering near his chair before bracing herself to take her leave. "Well. If it's all right with you, I'll be off now, Mr Parish." She turned and gave a little wave to the assembled company. "Goodnight!" she called.

To a chorus of 'Goodnights' she moved over to the door and came face to face with Mary, who had gone before her to open the door for her.

"Goodnight, Mrs Lampert," she said, moving past her through the open doorway. She stopped suddenly in her tracks as old Henry's voice boomed out.

"Just a minute!"

Startled almost out of her wits, she turned to face the old Judge, who was looking directly at her.

"You'd better come in and close the door, Nesta," he said quietly, and as she dutifully obliged and crossed over to him, continued: "Now I'm going to ask you a question." He peered directly into her eyes as he asked. "Do you think I'm an idiot?"

Completely thrown by the directness of his question, Nesta glanced anxiously around the room as she stammered, "Er . . . No . . . er . . . Oh, no, of course not, sir."

Henry smiled grimly and made an expansive gesture

to indicate all the others in the room.

"Well, everyone else around here has been treating me like a total imbecile, so I can tell you that you are in a minority of one." Nesta was looking utterly confused as Henry continued to hold the stage, informing her, "We've been playing a game of charades." He turned to Gerald, who was beginning to quake in his boots as his worst fears started to materialise. "Very appropriate under the circumstances, wouldn't you agree, Gerald?"

A thin, synthetic smile froze on Gerald's lips as he inclined his head forward to his father in an attitude of feigned innocence.

"Not quite catching your meaning, sir," he purred.

"Not wanting to, Gerald!" the old man barked. "You're praying to God I haven't really caught on. Well, I may be old and I may not be so quick off the mark as I used to be, but I'm not totally senile, as you're about to find out!" He paused to glance around the room at the anxious-looking faces staring silently back at him. "Bit of confusion in the ranks when I first arrived," he continued, addressing himself to Gerald. "First of all your secretary is telling me that I don't have any grandchildren, and then my supposed grandchildren give an excellent demonstration of being totally unaware that they have a grandfather, not to mention your supposed wife, who informs me that you never have meals with your fictitious family, because at that moment she had not yet been shown . . ." he took a note from his pocket and waved it before Gerald as he went on ". . . this note, which one of your supposed children left lying around." Henry paused as he unfolded the note, glanced at it and tossed it across to Gerald, smiling cynically as he commented, "You might like to keep it as a souvenir of the occasion." He then turned to Nesta. "And finally, a chorus of 'Goodnight Nestas' prompted you to say to her . . ." he nodded, indicating Mary, ". . . Goodnight Mrs Lampert."

His throat dry from his marathon performance, Henry handed his empty glass to Toby, saying, "Do you think you can pour some whisky into that without spilling it?"

Toby nodded as he took the glass and crossed over to the drinks table to fill it. Meanwhile, Henry turned and moved over to talk to Mary.

"Well, Mrs Lampert," he smiled. "What do you think I should do about the allowance I've been paying to Gerald?"

"Allowance?" She looked back at him questioningly. Henry had been watching her reaction closely, and it was fairly clear to him that she had no idea what he was talking about. He nodded towards Gerald as he began to explain.

"Wrote to me in desperation, seven years ago. Pleaded poverty. I wouldn't have given him a brass farthing, but I finally agreed to make him an allowance of ten thousand pounds a year to help support his family."

Incensed by the implication in the Judge's words, Mary retorted angrily, "We've never received a penny from Gerald!"

Henry put up his hands to placate her.

"I can quite believe it," he assured her. "Nevertheless," he went on, indicating Gerald, "he has received it from me and has done for seven years on the pretence that he was married with five children."

"I think that's disgusting!" she fumed, indignantly.

"Do you really?" Henry smiled, thoughtfully, turning to take his refilled glass of whisky from Toby. "Thank you, Toby." He took a sip from his glass, and chuckled quietly to himself before going on to say, "Funnily enough, I don't." As Mary turned to stare at him, he went on to explain. "I've always considered Gerald a total failure. He failed to follow in my footsteps and failed his Bar examinations, he's failed as a Solicitor, but my God, you've got to hand it to him. He's skived seventy thousand pounds out of me over the past few years, and if I hadn't come back to England, he might have had a lot more going into his bank account." He paused to take another sip from his glass, and there was a note of rueful admiration for his son as he reflected, "A liar he is. A cheat he is. But there isn't a court in the land that could touch him. I know! I was a Judge in the High Court!"

As she watched the old Judge, Mary relaxed a little as she began to appreciate his extraordinary reasoning, and she could see the twinkle in his eye as he turned to say, "Morally, he hasn't got a leg to stand on, but as far as the law is concerned, he's as pure as the driven snow." He chuckled. "He should be hanged, drawn and quartered, but when you get down to it, he's pulled off the 'con' of the century. He's taken us all for the proverbial ride and there's absolutely nothing any of us can do about it!"

He turned towards Gerald and raised his glass in a toast.

"Reluctantly, and with all the misgivings one could possibly imagine . . ." he beamed benevolently, "I drink a toast to my only son, Gerald Parish, who has turned out not to be quite such a failure after all."